H O T
LESBIAN
EROTICA

H O T
LESBIAN
EROTICA

Edited by

Tristan Taormino

CLEIS
PRESS

Published in the United States by Cleis Press Inc.,
P.O. Box 14697, San Francisco, California 94114.
Printed in the United States.
Cover design: Scott Idleman
Cover photograph: Celesta Danger
Text design: Frank Wiedemann
Cleis logo art: Juana Alicia
First Edition.
10 9 8 7 6 5 4 3 2 1

"Eighteen" © 2003 by Diane Thibault was previously published in *S.M.U.T.* magazine (October 2003); "An Australian Rodeo" © 2002 by Eva Hore was originally published on Storymistress.com (2002) and in *Delicate Friction* edited by Judith Bullock (2003); a different version of "Porta-Potty Passion" © 2004 by Sarah B. Wiseman previously appeared in *Hot & Bothered 3* edited by Karen X. Tulchinsky (Arsenal Pulp Press, 2001).

TABLE OF CONTENTS

Introduction
Tristan Taormino

What makes you hot? A handsome dyke in a sharp suit straightening her tie for you? A striking femme in a pair of fishnets and stilettos? A gentleman butch tipping your head back to plant a kiss on your luscious lips? How about the hungry look in your lover's eyes when she wants you? The feel of a firm hand tugging your hair? Or a soft leather collar being locked around your neck? Then there's that spot of wetness seeping through silk panties you discover as you undress her? Or the sight of boyish hips disappearing into a pair of striped boxer shorts? The smell of a woman's cunt when you first get your nose near it? The moment when her tongue makes contact with your sensitive clit—creating a spark so intense, it makes you catch your breath? Your hungry pussy sucking her fingers inside? Hers dripping around your hand? How it feels to be down on your knees looking up before your mouth is full? What she looks like with a cock between her legs as she pushes inside you? Her hands cupping your ass? The weight of her against you?

Heat can be a tricky thing. There is the kind of heat you

can feel between you—the heat that rises off bodies, warm and thick and palpable. There's heat that flushes your skin. Heat that induces sweat, makes cotton T-shirts stick to your chest, soaks your body. A heat that sends your heart racing, leaves you panting, grunting, even yelling. Or a heat that consumes you, overwhelms you, nearly suffocates you, makes it hard to think. There are lots of different kinds of heat.

What about a private striptease show from your girlfriend? A mysterious stranger who's good with her hands? A hot dyke behind the wheel ready to take you for a ride? That's just a taste of what's between the pages of this collection. Here, you'll find plenty of hot women, including a Daddy in the lingerie dressing room of a department store and a small-town cop with a submissive side. Here are horny writers whose stories inspire, confident butches with ulterior motives, and high-priced lesbian call girls. A famous tennis player supervises her eager landscaper, a gentleman rescues a damsel in distress, and an uppity girl makes trouble just to get punished. Hot women in even hotter scenarios, like: an amusement park tryst, an older woman's crush on a much younger dyke, a secret two A.M. rendezvous, a game that ends with one player on her back in the grass. Hot women in even hotter places having scorching sex. Sex on a waterbed, sex on a subway train, sex in a porta-potty, sex in a bookstore, and sex in a restaurant. Rough rodeo sex, reigniting sex, reunion sex. Scorching sex that feeds egos, quenches thirsts, pushes boundaries, seduces straight girls, and heals relationships.

So go ahead and embrace the heat. Let it take over. There will be time for cool baths, spinning fans, and buzzing air conditioners later.

Tristan Taormino
New York City
February 14, 2005

Trick with a Match
Alison Smith

The summer I graduated from college I took a job as a line cook working the evening shift at a diner right off the interstate. We served mostly truckers and vagrants. We had a lot of regulars and the waitresses copped an attitude. If you ordered chocolate cream pie and they brought you apple, you ate it anyway, and it was best not to say anything. The girl who worked prep table was named Danni. She was good with a knife, and fast, and I liked that. I had worked my way through college as a prep cook at a Boy Scout camp, so I could tell a lot about a person by the way she handled a knife.

All night, we were pressed up against each other in the narrow space behind the counter, the heat rising off the grease-slick grill, and I couldn't help but notice certain things about Danni. She palmed the vegetables, rolling them between her hands for a moment before she cut them. It was as if she had to get to know them first. I had never seen that before. She carried a pack of imported matches—Swan Vestas from England—in an oversized side pocket of her pants. She had one dimple, on the left cheek. It became more prominent when she smiled, which was not often. And one of her shoulders was higher than the other.

"Paper route," she said when she caught me looking at her lopsided stance. "I always carried my sack of newspapers on the same side."

"Why didn't you alternate?" I asked.

Her eyes followed the line of my kitchen apron from my chest to my waist, down to its gravy-stained edge just past my knees. "Alternate." She said it slowly. She nodded and pursed her lips. "Hear that, Mico?" she called over her shoulder. "College girl wants to know why I didn't alternate."

Mico was the busboy.

The onions made her cry. She wiped the tears off her cheek with the back of her hand, the knife's silver handle gleaming against her palm. The previous cook had taught her to hold a match between her teeth. He said the sulfur would cut the sting. It didn't work, but she still held the match in her mouth every night. It dangled between her lips like a toothpick. I watched her teeth work against the wooden tip as tears smeared across her cheeks.

She had a trick she'd do with the match. When she finished cutting the onions, she'd light it, then turn it backward with a flick of her teeth against her tongue until the lit end disappeared inside her mouth. For a split second her hollowed cheeks glowed. Then she closed her lips and the flame died.

It was a silly, circus trick, but under the dull fluorescents, the wan night winding by, the endless line of coffee mugs and burger plates, the trick with the match caught our attention. The regulars beat the counter and chanted, "Eat the match." They cheered when her cheeks glowed. They dared her to swallow the match ends. The waitresses rolled their eyes and told her she was going to burn her insides someday. They didn't like anything that took attention away from them. I pressed the juice out of the burgers and watched her mouth, the pale, glowing cheeks.

It was an all-night diner. WE NEVER CLOSE was its motto, and for the most part it was true. But once a month, on a Sunday, they locked the doors at midnight and we stayed inside to clean and restock. The waitresses wouldn't work if there were no tips, so the chores were left to the cook staff and the busboys. On those nights, Danni was in charge. Mostly, I just cleaned my grill and poured the grease out in the back lot. I let them take care of the rest. It was supposed to be a summer job; I had told the owner I couldn't stay past September, and Danni said she didn't see the point of training me in restocking if I was just going to up and leave.

But in late October, the frost already creeping across my car windshield at night, I was still there. That Sunday she sent Mico and Stan—the other busboy—home early. She said she'd rather do it alone than deal with them any longer. They were out the door in two seconds. One of her jobs was to refill the ketchup jars from the dispenser in the basement. She grabbed the bottles off the tables and balanced a tray of them on her shoulder. I asked her if she wanted help. She shifted her weight toward me and said, "No," then, "Yes," then, "All right."

Light from the kitchen spilled halfway down the basement stairs. I followed her and watched as she disappeared into the darkness. I had only been in the basement a handful of times. The busboys kept my station well stocked. They knew where everything was in the walk-in cooler. It was easier for them to get it than to explain where to find it. So when she asked me to turn on the light in the basement, I couldn't locate the switch. She set the tray down and watched me in the darkness, running my hand along the wall, groping for the light switch. She didn't offer to help. She pulled the Vestas out of her pocket.

"Want me to show you how to do it?" she asked.

I turned away from her. "I don't like that trick," I said.

She grabbed my arm at the wrist and pulled a match out with her free hand. I tried to wrench my arm away. She squeezed harder. She lit the match by running the tip along the zipper of her pants and placed it between her teeth. Her head tilted back so that the flame flickered straight up, away from her face. "Now watch," she said. Her tongue darted out. The bottom teeth slid forward. She let the match flip back into the cave of her mouth. Her cheeks glowed even brighter in the dark basement. Then she closed her lips. The match went out. She released my arm.

"Now you try," she said. She held a fresh match out for me.

I looked down at her sneakers. I shook my head.

"You scared?" she asked.

"No," I said. I rubbed my wrist where she had held it. "I just think there are better things you could do with your time."

"Like what, college girl?" She put her hands on my shoulders. I felt them pressing against the cotton T-shirt, felt their warmth. She shoved me and I stumbled back. My foot caught on an empty box and I went down. My head hit the corner of the supply shelves, and I found myself on the floor with sugar packets raining down around me. I rubbed my head. Danni stood above me, laughing.

I scrambled to my feet and pitched myself at her. I had little experience with fighting. I had never flown at someone like that before. She caught me easily and pushed my weight past her, but she didn't let me go. If she had, I would have crashed against the stairs. Instead, she bound both my wrists in one of her hands. She held them behind my back. She opened her mouth, plucked the spent match off her tongue, and flicked it onto the floor. She just stood there holding my wrists, staring at me. We were breathing hard. I listened to the sound of our breath rasping through us. Then she shrugged and released my wrists. Instead of stepping away from me, she moved closer. I could feel her breath on my neck.

She whispered in my ear, "What are you going to do now, college girl?"

I kissed her. I started taking off her clothes. I got pretty far before she stopped me. She wouldn't let me take off her bra. When I reached for the clasp, she folded her arms across her chest and shook her head. It is the bra I remember most clearly. It was not what I expected. It was white cotton with eyelet trim. The fabric had lost its brightness, its elasticity, and it held her loosely in its fragile cups. She let me push her up on the metal table. The tray of bottles crashed to the floor. I looked over at them. She grabbed my face and pulled me back to her. I kissed her again and pushed her up further onto the table.

I slipped one finger inside of her, ran my tongue over my middle finger, and slipped that in too. I remember the delicious smoothness of her. She felt endless. She asked me if I wanted to fist her. My fingers went still inside her. I had never done it before. I stared at the wall behind the table and said, "Yes." It was as if the word were written there, on the basement wall next to the ketchup dispenser. *Yes, yes.*

She put her feet on my shoulders and pointed at her pants, now crumpled on the table beside us. She told me to open the side pocket.

"The matches?" I asked.

"No, the other pocket."

There I found a dented, eight-ounce bottle of Probe. I made a joke, told her she should be a Boy Scout. She looked at me. I nodded at the bottle, "Because you're always prepared." She didn't laugh and it was then that I knew she had planned this.

She talked me into her, from the first finger to the fourth. My fingers formed not a fist so much as a cup, a shallow bowl inside her. We ran out of lube just before the knuckle.

"Keep going," she said. She was breathing hard now, and I watched the top of her breasts move against the frayed eyelet of her bra. Her body pulled me in and my hand—poised and trembling—followed. I kissed the edge of my palm and watched it disappear inside her. My fingertips rested against her cervix and then curled into a fist.

"It's in," she said.

I nodded.

She let her head drop back for a moment. The sweat dampened the fine hair around her temples. "It's in," she repeated, her South Boston accent growing stronger.

For a little while I stayed there, quiet, unmoving. I watched as she moved against me, rocking against my wrist. A hunger grows in you when you put your hand in a girl, and I wanted her to want me to stay there. I watched her face. I watched as her hips rose and slid closer to me, toward the edge of the table. I wanted to do this right. My free hand moved over my own small breasts, then onto hers, fingering the edge of the bra. I started to perspire and shiver at the same time. I bent my elbow and moved closer to her, wrapped my other hand around her neck, and pulled her mouth toward mine. She let me kiss her and then said, "I think you can fuck harder than that." I let go of her neck and her head dropped onto the table.

I got one knee up on the table for better leverage. I moved my fist up toward the front of her, toward the place where I had been told the G-spot was. She liked that. I felt her grow wetter, smoother. I started to move with her. My hand pressed further into her. Her feet slipped off my shoulders and hovered, weightless, in the air behind me. She held the edge of the table. She started begging me for it, for more of me. I was ready to climb all the way inside her if that was what it took. The table was shaking against the wall, my free arm trembled, but I kept my fist inside her, steady and even. She covered her eyes with her hands. She called out my proper name—I didn't even know she knew it. Her back arched. She let out a cry and pulled me down on top of her.

Her body convulsed under me, shaking us both. I held the edge of the table to keep us from falling. As soon as her breathing slowed, she pushed herself up on her elbows and stared at my wrist where it disappeared inside her, searching for a glimpse of the lost hand.

Outside, smoke from a pile of smoldering leaves in the yard next door curled into the wind. The sharp smell of her mingled with the scent of burning leaves. A car drove past with its windows down. We heard the muffled whine of the stereo. A street lamp curved out above us toward the road. It caught the shape of her long face, the one dimple. I nodded toward the parking lot and asked if I could give her a ride home. I told her I could put her bike in the trunk.

"No thanks, college girl." She turned and walked away from me, around the back of the building. I stood there in the darkness and listened till I heard the sound of the chain rasping against the bike frame. Then I pulled the keys out of my pocket and walked toward my car.

Pratfall
Betty Blue

Emma was five-feet-ten-inches of trouble. She was trouble on legs any idiot would have seen coming; it would take a special kind of idiot not to. But it just so happens that I am that kind of special.

She had a smile like the Cheshire Cat, left lingering in the air long after she'd graced you with it and gone her way. Ruby-washed lips that looked as if she'd been sucking on cherry ice parted over a nearly perfect set of teeth, but for a snaggle tooth that gave the impression she was smirking. And maybe she was. Yeah, you bet she was.

You could say that the trouble that was Emma just landed in my lap. Luckily, I have enough lap for that. She was carrying an armload of boxes balanced in front of her, bounding down the steps of the apartment building I was looking to move into when she tripped on the last step and came straight for me, boxes and incredible limbs flying like an early test-run at Kitty Hawk. I caught her and stumbled back, falling onto my ass on the (thankfully) deserted sidewalk. Emma landed on top of me, taking my breath away in both the near literal and the dopey, metaphoric fools-fall-in-love kind of way. Candy-apple red curls covered my face and the rest of her covered everything else.

I took this as a good omen for the rental situation.

She apologized profusely as she disentangled her limbs, and I, of course, took one look at those dangerous green eyes and that cherry-ice-stain Cheshire smile, and was hooked, line and sinker.

"No," I insisted, running my hand across the back of my neck through the soft, close-shorn hair my ex-girlfriend used to refer to as "puppy tummy" for the way it felt against her hand. It was a nervous habit, like pushing my glasses up my nose in a Christopher Reeve Superman kind of way. (I am just full of that kind of charm.) "It was my fault. I shouldn't have been, um, standing there." I coughed nervously, looking down at my boots and jingling change in my pocket, and Emma let out a peal of laughter that made my cunt quiver. I was definitely taking this apartment.

"I'm Emma," she said. "Fuck me." Or probably she didn't say that; it was most likely something like "Buckley." But a girl hears what she wants to hear. And then she said the thing that ruined the entire building for me. "I'm moving out."

"Oh," I said. (I'm clever with words that way.)

I got up and was helping her out of her pile of boxes when Emma made another one of those dangerous sounds. This time it was a squeal, and it burst out of her as she fell into my arms, and I thought, *damn, girl, am I good*, and then realized she was grimacing with pain.

"Shit," she said, hopping on one really long, really fabulous leg in a pair of loose cut-off sweats. "I think I twisted my ankle." She leaned against me and turned to look at her scattered boxes. "Dammit. How am I going to get all my stuff down to the truck?"

Anybody else would have realized from the loud, cork-popping sound that that minute's sucker was being born.

"I can carry some stuff down for you," I said. "I'm really early for my appointment, so I've got lots of time."

She flashed me the snaggle tooth to seal the deal. "Oh, would you? Oh, my God, you're a life-saver!"

Her U-Haul was waiting in front of the building, and I loaded the boxes into the back while she sat on the steps nursing her ankle, and then helped her back up the stairs to her apartment. While she reclined on the couch with a bag of frozen peas on her ankle, I took stock of the apartment. There weren't any boxes waiting to be moved, which might have seemed suspicious if I hadn't been taking lesbian inventory. She had the right collection of books—*Odd Girls and Twilight Lovers; Our Bodies, Ourselves; Macho Sluts*—some tasteful black-and-white nudes on the wall, a Bettie Page calendar. The signs were favorable.

"It's just the computer, the stereo, and the TV and DVD player," said Emma, drawing my focus back to her ruby-stained mouth. "And then I've got some stuff in the bedroom...some clothes, some other stuff." She flashed the snaggle tooth. "You have no idea what a terrific favor this is...." She paused, waiting for me to fill in the blank.

"Cal," I supplied.

"Cal." Emma smiled as though she liked the feel of my name in her mouth. "Seriously, Cal, you have no idea. I'll owe you big."

That was enough to get me moving, hoisting electronic equipment as fast as I could down the two flights of stairs and out to the truck. When I'd finished the living room, I came back upstairs to find Emma in her bedroom, rummaging through the closet and tossing things in a box next to the bed. She threw a pair of shoes over her shoulder and into the box that held an assortment of more interesting odds and ends.

"Wow," I said in that clever way I have, peeking into the

box. "That's a lot of vibrators."

Emma laughed and stood up, hopping back to drop onto the bed in front of the box containing a Hitachi, a Sunbeam, and a Wahl on top of an assortment of battery-operated Smoothies and overdesigned Japanese "pearls."

"It's always good to have a backup," she said with a grin. She picked up the Wahl and unplugged the cord. "This one's really great, but sometimes it runs out of juice before I do." Emma flicked on the switch and it began to hum invitingly. "It's rechargeable, so you don't have to worry about the cord, but I always forget to plug it back in when I'm done, and then it quits on me, so I've got my other options." She took my hand and pressed the humming vibrator against my palm.

"Yeah," I stammered. "That one's good."

"Feel free to try it anywhere you like," said Emma with that smile.

Even I am not too stupid to pick up on an invitation like that. But I made one last attempt at pretending I had not come up to the apartment of a virtual stranger and helped her haul equipment down two flights of stairs in hopes of getting some.

I looked at my watch. "I'm supposed to meet my new roommate downstairs in thirty minutes," I said. Emma only blinked at me. There. I'd done my moral duty; that was enough of that. "So…where do *you* like it?"

Emma took my hand and slipped it down the front of her drawstring sweats, the string just tight enough to hold me there. If you've ever made candy, there's a point at which the confection is beaten to a high gloss, just before it becomes firm, like a handful of stiff silk. A very recent and impeccable Brazilian wax had left Emma's cunt feeling like candy.

"There, huh?" I said quietly. "Right there?" I moved my fingers into the soft ribbon of her confection.

Emma let out a soft breath and leaned back across the bed,

the Wahl still beating like a frantic heart in her hand. I teased down the edge of her sweats barely to her thighs, revealing the sweet prize beneath my palm. The tips of her lips were glistening, and nestled between them, like a door knocker on her clit, was a bright steel ring with a pearl for a captive bead—steeped in Victorian romantic metaphor in case anyone might not be able to find what they were looking for. But I found it with no trouble at all.

I pried open her pussy and moistened my finger with her own slippery fluids, stroking the dampness against the shaft of her clit as I crawled over her. Emma reached up and slipped her hands beneath my shirt, just skirting the underslope of my breasts as she ran her hands behind me and pulled me down on top of her. I lost my place where I'd been exploring below.

"Hi," I said, looking into those deadly green eyes.

"Hi," she said, grinning.

Emma reached up and pulled off my glasses, thus ensuring that I would be doing more searching with my fingers, and then caught my mouth with hers. As she nipped my lower lip with her teeth, I jumped in surprise at the sudden sensation at my cunt. She had slipped the cordless vibe between the two of us and begun to rock, driving it into me with her rhythm so that even through my jeans, the vibration was intense. We moaned into each other's mouths and I hung on to her hair as we swayed and creaked against each other's bodies like waves against a ship's hull, pressing, pressing, swaying, surging.

She came first, with a fabulous shriek and shudder, while I followed a few moments later with a soft-rising crescendo, orgasm muted by cloth.

"Oh, we can do better than that," she whispered against my ear. She let the vibrator fall unheeded and jittery against the bedspread while she slipped my belt from its buckle and threaded her fingers deftly through the buttons of my fly, hustling my jeans down around my knees. Her fingers pressed into my cunt insistently, finding a slick reception and no pro-test. "We can do much better than that," she said, and began to pump her warm fingers expertly inside me in a teasing, but quickening, staccato.

"Oh, fuck!" I gasped, burying my head in her jasmine-scented neck.

"That *is* the idea," she agreed, her voice deep, fingers pumping harder, then stopping and starting again in short, sharp bursts.

I fumbled at the buttons of her white, cotton "boyfriend" shirt, gasping and jerking at her orchestration between my legs. Emma was braless beneath the well-worn cotton and I dipped my mouth quickly to one of her pink-tipped breasts, cupping the other breast in my hand, giving her a little com-petition as she tried to maintain her skillful concentration. She moaned and fucked me harder when I drew the taut nipple between my teeth, and I twisted uncontrollably on her jolting fingers, driving her further into me, letting go to pant help-lessly against her damp nipple as she deftly added her thumb to the onslaught. She pressed tight against my clit, kneading it in a circular motion, her other hand under my T-shirt releas-ing one tit to pinch the nipple, until I cried out and came thunderously within the unrelenting embrace of her hand.

As I relaxed against her, I heard the Wahl jumping against the bedspread.

Emma laughed and I rolled aside as she clutched around for it on the bed. The vibrator started to make a whining, depressed sort of noise as she found it, and she held it up as it petered out with a sad little sotto voce shudder. "See? What did I tell you? Left it unplugged too long while I was packing. It really sucks, because this is the only thing that really makes me come."

"Oh, I bet there are one or two things that could beat it," I said mischievously, and slipped down off the side of the bed before she could stop me, prowling over her lap and slipping my tongue between her legs.

Emma squealed, but made no move to stop me—pressing up to meet me, in fact, white tennis shoes dangling on either side of me over the edge of the bed. The sweats were still trapped at her thighs, but she seemed to like the restricting sensation, straining against it just enough to make the drawstring bite into her flesh as I braced my hands on her hips and buried my face in her pussy.

An old Echo & The Bunnymen song raced through my head as I tasted her, in keeping with the candy theme of her confection-smooth cunt: *Lips like sugar.* I was lost in the pleasure of it for my own sake, pressing my tongue through her clit ring and stroking the head beneath its slick hood. Emma arched up against my eager mouth, filling me with the sugar of her cunt and making soft noises between her teeth. I drove my tongue in deeper, tracing upward from her ass, tight in the grip of the restricting shorts, up in a swift, straight stroke, and then down again, plunging into her cunt, my lips against her clit and my teeth dragging the ring against it. Emma began to shake, her moans keeping time with my tongue. When I brought my hand up from the box on the floor and slid the Japanese dildo with its rotating pearls into the hot, willing hollow, Emma threw back her head with a shout and thrust down on my hand, fucking herself desperately against it as she came. The whole building had to have heard her as she thrashed against me, shouting, "Oh, fuck! Oh, god! Oh, Cal!" It couldn't have hurt my reputation as a new tenant.

I laughed against her damp lips as I pulled the dildo gently out of her. "Well, that was disappointing," I said, kissing her thighs. "We should have gone with the Wahl."

"Oh, shut *up!*" she laughed, struggling to sit up and coming up on her elbows. The clock on the nightstand came into her view. "Shit," she said. "I've gotta be out of here in five minutes."

I groped for my glasses, wiping my mouth on the back of my hand. "My appointment's at noon," I said.

"Yeah. Five minutes." Emma scrambled to right her clothing while I hoisted my jeans back over my hips. "This is the last box," she said, tossing the damp pearl dildo and the now-dead Wahl in on top of the pile of vibrators. "And that suitcase by the door." She gave me an apologetic look, flashing the snaggle-tooth smile. "I hate to give you the bum's rush."

"Don't worry about it," I said, giving her a kiss as I took the box from her. "I have to get down there and meet Beth anyway. Wouldn't want to make a bad first impression."

Emma had stood up and taken a step toward the door, and she made a sharp gasp as her weight rested on the twisted ankle.

"Here," I said, catching her under one arm. "Just lean on me and grab the suitcase."

"You are a life-saver, Cal. Did I mention that?" The green eyes, the ruby-washed lips, and the smile all worked together at once, making my cunt jump in a little aftershock of remembrance of the past half hour.

I got her safely down to her truck, all packed up, by 11:59. Emma hopped up into the driver's seat without a wince. I frowned. No, she couldn't have been faking it. It was mean and uncharitable of me to even think it.

"You're the best, Cal," she called out the window as she pulled away. "You have no idea what you did for me today!"

The U-Haul rounded a corner and disappeared. That was a first; dykes I've just met are usually driving the other way. I walked back to the steps with a sigh, realizing too late that there had been no exchange of numbers. Maybe I could get her number from someone else in the building.

"Are you Cal?" I looked up to see my prospective new roommate approaching, smiling and holding out her hand. We had done our negotiating over the phone, but hadn't yet met in person. "I'm Beth. Come on up. I'll show you the place."

I followed Beth up the stairs with a guilty thrill at what I'd just been doing in the building. We went up one flight of stairs, then two, then stopped in front of a door. Emma's door.

"Oh, wow," I stammered.

"What?" said Beth, turning the key.

"I think I just helped your old roommate move out."

Beth paused at the door. "My old roommate? I didn't have a—oh, don't tell me Emma was here."

I reddened. "I think she said that was her name."

"Shit," said Beth. "She's my ex. She told me she'd stop by to pick up a few things. I hope she didn't give you a hard time."

"No, not a hard time," I said as Beth opened the door. It figured. My new roommate's ex.

Beth stopped in the hallway and stared at the living room and the empty entertainment center. "*No.*" She turned and looked around the room. "Oh, she did *not! My computer?*"

"Oh. Shit." I ran the whole morning in my head, from the comical fall that could not have landed better had it been planned, to the sprained ankle that did not seem to bother Emma once she was out the door, to the sweating, frantic fuck on what must be Beth's bed. I had just fucked my new roommate's ex, and then robbed her blind.

Beth ran down the hall and into the bedroom, and I followed with sinking dread, certain she was going to take one look at the bed and realize what had happened in here. I tried to think of something to say that would make me sound like less of an ass. Maybe capitalize on that special idiot quality of mine.

"No, no, *no!*" Beth was crouched by the bed, the covers thrown off in a heap so she could look beneath it. She straightened and flopped onto the mattress with an angry bounce. "I can't believe it." Beth closed her eyes and put her hands on either side of her head. "The bitch stole my vibrators."

Behind Beth on the headboard was a picture of the two of them that I hadn't noticed before. Emma stared out of the frame, arms around Beth with her chin on Beth's head. Her cherry-ice-stained, snaggle-tooth, Cheshire Cat smile gave the impression she was smirking. And maybe she was. Yeah, you bet she was.

Just Another Day at the Beach
Rachel Kramer Bussel

It was the middle of summer, and my girlfriend Jill and I had taken a long weekend to relax and enjoy the sun, and each other. Our jobs don't cut us much slack, so it was mid-August before we had our first real chance to get away. She'd never been to the beach with me so she had no clue what to expect. She probably thought she'd simply slather on some cocoa butter, indulge in a meaty paperback, and swim till she became exhausted. She'd be exhausted, all right, by the end of the day—but not from sitting around. We'd borrowed our friend's keys to the secluded, members-only beach, so our privacy would be guaranteed.

I settled into my chair and watched as she went through her elaborate beach ritual, her body snug in her new Pucci print bikini, pushing her tits out until you'd have to be blind not to see them. She slowly oiled herself, moving up one arm, down the next, all over her exposed chest and cute stomach. She bent forward, treating me to a view of her perfect ass as she slathered the white liquid onto her toes, ankles, and calves. I had to shift in my seat as she kept going, her brow furrowed as she tried to get every last spot, contorting this way and that as her hand reached behind to get her back. Seeing her ass sticking right out in front of me, so perfect she could be a model, I sat on my hands in order not to reach out and squeeze those precious cheeks. Usually when she bends over like that, it's so I can give her a nice, hard smack.

I crossed my legs in the chair and felt my pussy contract. Watching her is my favorite spectator sport. She loves to tan, and often steals a few hours of sun on our roof in the mornings. In preparation for this outing, she'd tried on swimsuit after swimsuit, modeling the barely-there materials that accentuated every bulging, glistening curve.

I had opted for a simple black one-piece, a low-maintenance suit that doesn't cause me any trouble and still emphasizes the right parts of my body. I held back a smile as I watched Jill twist and turn to rub lotion on her back, first going over her shoulder, then behind her and around. I had plans to keep her on her back for most of the afternoon, but she didn't need to know that yet. "Come here," I beckoned, and she did, sheepishly handing me the bottle. I had her sit between my legs and lean forward, then poured a healthy amount of lotion onto her back and started kneading it in, not simply rubbing but pounding it into her with my palms. As I pressed harder and harder, my hands roaming from her shoulder blades to the small of her back, she let out a moan. I pushed her head down and squeezed the back of her neck, pinching and pressing that delicate skin. I brought all my weight to bear, focusing on her neck and shoulders, feeling her go limp. I knew she was getting turned on, but I pretended not to and went about my business until her back was fully slathered with sunscreen.

I skimmed my fingertips down her back, lightly tickling her, then whispered into her ear, "You didn't really need so much sunscreen on your back, you know. I don't think it'll be facing the sun for too long today…though I could be wrong."

She turned her head and squinted at me but didn't say a word. She knew exactly what I meant, and I in turn knew that she'd agree to whatever I asked of her. That arrangement's worked quite well for the eight months we'd been together, and neither of us has stopped getting a little thrill of arousal when I give her an order. "Put on the sun mask," I told her, liking how this toy doubled as a blindfold. It's better for her to be slightly surprised, I thought, to have to wait in the darkness before I ravished her. I let her lie out in the sun for half an hour, let it beam its searing rays down on her, at the hottest time of day, her eyes hidden behind the mask. Finally, my timer buzzed and I dragged her into the shade. "Can I go in the water?" she asked, her skin warm to the touch.

"In a little while," I demurred, and had her lie down. "I have a better way to cool you off," I said, pulling her to me and kissing her, our lips pressing frantically together as I reached my hand between her legs. Immediately, she whimpered.

"Please, Alex, please," is all she said as I played with her beneath the thin barrier of her bikini bottom. She spread her legs and I pressed harder against her, then gave her pussy a light tap and watched her body jolt. I let out a huge breath as I imagined pulling her suit aside to see her gorgeous pussy lips.

Quietly as I could, I grabbed some ice from the cooler. then let a few drops of freezing water fall onto her skin. She squirmed and tried to move but I knelt on top of her, straddling her as I brought the ice toward her skin, running it along her neck and over her breasts, lingering on her nipples until they stood out, hard and beaded. She whimpered, and I took advantage of her open mouth to slide the half-melted cube inside. I rubbed another cube over her bikini bottom, icing it up before sliding the ice all the way down one leg, then back up, doing the same with the other. I let her finish the cube in her mouth, sucking on it deliciously. "Are you still ready?" I teased her as I peeled off her bikini, slowly dragging it down her legs. In response, she spread her legs, showing me the pussy that never fails to elicit a raw, animalistic urge to fuck her. I moved so that my own cunt was balanced on my heel, grinding against my foot as I held open her lips with one hand and rubbed an ice cube against her opening with the other. She gasped and tried to squirm away, and when I removed the cube, she cried out.

"Keep going, please, Alex, I need it," she begged. I slid the cube up and down her already slippery slit, pressing it against her clit before sliding it lower and then pushing it inside. I played with the ice, rubbing it against her inner walls and watching as the water dripped out of her, feeling her squeeze my fingers on this frozen delight.

"Good girl," I told her, and that phrase, with my fingers slamming into her, was enough to set her off into a roaring orgasm, her whole body shaking as she clutched me for dear life. I rode it out with her, pressing my own heel against my tingling cunt, aroused beyond belief.

Now I was getting her where I wanted her. The sun was making me feel delirious. "Okay, bathing beauty, now it's time for a little contest. Well, you're the only contestant—but I still expect you to do be an excellent performer." I sat in the chair, mustering all the height and haughtiness I could. I looked her up and down like a sleazy judge at a cheap beauty contest. "Come over here and turn around for me." She complied by strutting around, even bending over, showing off her curvy ass. I gave her butt a light squeeze, then made her put her bikini bottom back on and handed her a skimpy shirt. "We're going to have a wet T-shirt contest now, so I need you to take off your top, put on this shirt, and then get in the water. You'll be judged like in the Olympics, on a scale of one to ten, with points for clinginess, sex appeal, and originality. You can do whatever you want as long as you keep your T-shirt on. And before you even ask, you will be highly rewarded for a high score—trust me on that." I could see her eyes light up, her mind churning as she tried to figure out how she could dazzle me. "I'll be sitting right over here," I said, pointing.

We were practically touching, and she batted her eyes at me the way she always does to get what she wants. "Can I really do whatever I want as long as I keep my T-shirt on?" she asked, putting on a simpering manner. She sure knew how to drive me crazy, and I almost bagged the whole thing, scooped her up over my shoulder, and brought her home, but I came to my senses in time. This would be too much fun to miss out on.

"That's what I said. Now get moving." I gently swatted her away, then settled into my chair, a magazine over my lap and one hand idly playing with my clit underneath it. She knew that I was really putty in her manicured hands, but we both went along with the charade that I was in charge. She loped off toward the ocean, and after a while I couldn't see her any-more. I tried to read my magazine but couldn't concentrate, and instead closed my eyes, picturing what Jill would look like with that flimsy little shirt clinging to her tits. I didn't have to wait long, because before I knew it, drops of water were falling onto me. I looked up and got quite the shock—she was standing in front of me wearing *only* the shirt, which left nothing to the imagination. I looked up and saw her holding her wet bikini bottom in front of me, and breathed a sigh of relief that we were in such a private area, or my little bad girl might have gotten us arrested.

She thrust her chest out toward me, teasing me with her protruding nipples. I felt a throbbing in my cunt, but I let her go on with her show. She bent over and spread her legs so that I could see her pussy lips right in front of me, then turned around and used her yoga training to do a handstand. Then she walked over and planted herself between my legs, pushing her barely covered nipples right into my face before pulling the fabric apart with her hands. It tore straight down the middle so I was left facing her large breasts, the few drops of saltwater remaining on them quickly drying in the sun's rays as she gave me the sexiest lap dance imaginable.

"Wow," was all I could say, looking up at her in awe. I'd underestimated my star girl, thinking she'd be too shy for this, but I should have known better. Jill never met a challenge, especially a sexy one, that she couldn't beat. "Okay, you win. Ten out of ten. Are you ready for your reward?" She preened in front of me.

"I don't know. Are you?" she tossed back. So I grabbed her, lifting her up into my arms as she laughed hysterically. I brought her back to the chair and managed to lay her across my lap without both of us toppling over.

"Your prize is a nice, hard spanking, one worthy of a girl who gets a perfect score. What do you think about that?" I asked as I squeezed her asscheeks, pinching them and spreading them apart, teasing her as I prolonged her spanking. I pretended to accidentally brush my knuckle across her exposed pussy, finding her deliciously wet. She moaned and I pushed two fingers into her mouth for her to suckle as I started spanking that perfect little ass. The sound was loud, a perfect echo. With only a few smacks I made her cheeks bright red. Her mouth was frantically sucking on my fingers, and then, as I increased the force of my smacks, she bared her teeth, and I knew I'd have marks on my fingers once we were done. I didn't mind, though, for it gave me the chance to turn that gorgeous ass into my own personal easel. I raised my hand as high as I could and brought it down on her ass, almost toppling us as she moaned against my fingers. I pinched the part of her ass nearest her pussy, then tapped my fingers against her swollen lips.

Finally, I took pity on her and plunged three fingers into her cunt, smiling as they slid inside in a flash. I pressed down, twisting my fingers, hardly needing to do a thing since she was already so worked up. I slid a fourth finger into her, teasing her clit with my thumb, and pulled my soggy fingers out of her mouth to grab a fistful of her windblown hair. I could feel her getting close and started moving faster, my fingers grinding into her as deeply as I could manage. Then there it was, her climax, like a shock to both our systems as she shuddered beneath me.

After a few moments we came back to earth. She looked up at me, squinting. "Baby, I just have one question," she said. "I know I got a perfect score, but can we have a wet T-shirt contest next time we go to the beach?"

"Of course," I said, and kissed her. We'd be fools not to.

Under the Boardwalk
Nipper Godwin

Pop tunes from the '60s had been running through her head all day long—it was that kind of place. The amusement park looked seedy and rundown, many of the rides bearing CLOSED FOR REPAIRS signs across locked gates. Even the barkers at the wheel-of-fortune booths seemed tired. Despite that, a glimmer of excitement lingered, left over from the park's glory days. This had been Mel's favorite place in the world, when she was a kid at the Jersey shore, for there was no Disney World, no Six Flags, nothing but Coney Island to compare it to, all those years ago. Janey stood beside the splintery railing with her back to the beach, shielding her eyes against the sun that was setting on the hot June day like a big red rubber ball.

Mel waved from across the half-empty parking lot. She had a bundle under one arm.

"What, you want to lie on the sand and make out?" Janey asked with a smile, taking the blanket.

The corners of Mel's eyes crinkled into laugh lines. "Better than that," she said, taking Janey's hand. "Come on!"

Their footsteps drummed a syncopated beat down the

ramp. No attendant was posted at the top to check permit buttons, this late in the day. Janey took her hand back and pulled off her sandals before setting out into the deep sand. When she looked back up, her lover was scanning the beach.

"It's empty," Janey remarked. There were only a few die-hard sunbathers on blankets, widely scattered. A guy with a metal detector paced slowly down the strand, a few hundred feet away.

"Too early in the season," Mel explained, leading her back toward the pier in the shadow of the boardwalk.

Over the crash of the surf, Janet could hear the distant clatter and roar of the roller coaster, the sound of its screaming riders faint and small as in a dream. She thought she could hear the calliope, too, for just a moment over the wind, but they'd already seen that the merry-go-round was closed, the great painted horses still in the center of the deserted penny arcade. Ghost music, she thought. The smell of cotton candy, just a faint whiff carried away on the sea breeze, was real enough.

Mel stopped to peer down the sand at two small children conferring over the castle they were building with bright-colored plastic buckets, just out of reach of the waves. Their voices were too far away to hear. As soon as their backs were turned, Mel grabbed Janey's hand again. "Here," she said, ducking under the huge beam and past the silver-gray piling that held up one side of the broad walkway overhead.

The sand there felt cool under her feet, and the air smelled of seaweed and creosote, out of the wind. The surf, instantly muted, became nothing but a dull distant shushing. Janey watched Mel as she bent to spread the blanket, careful not to hit her head as she straightened back up. Her grin flashed white in the dim light.

"After you," she said, gesturing. Janey sat carefully, smoothing her skirt under her and trying not to get sand on the olive-drab army blanket.

Mel settled in next to her. Golden light poured through a knothole, too bright to look at. Out on the beach, the sand was sunset orange and the strip of visible sea was a dark gray-blue. Janey looked at her beloved's face, letting her eyes adjust to the darkness. In the bright noonday sun, the sand would be striped with lines of light and the spaces between the boards overhead would be dazzling, Janey knew. The still air would feel stifling. They wouldn't have the place to themselves, either, she thought, imagining the twined bodies of young lovers in the shadows. More ghosts. She pulled her sweater tighter around her.

"Are you cold?" Mel untied the hooded sweatshirt from her waist and snuggled close, draping it over them both.

"Not any more," Janey said, her lover's breath warm on her cheek. Mel covered her mouth with a kiss. She tasted salty, like buttered popcorn, with a hint of candy-apple sweetness. Janey wondered if she herself still carried the flavor of the blue raspberry Sno-Cone she had licked earlier. Mel's tongue slipped past her lips, hot and insistent. She gave herself up to sensation, feeling Mel's soft lips pressing hers, their tongues twining, feeling as if she were opening up, growing warm between her legs.

They paused, holding their breath, to listen to footsteps ringing hollow from the boards overhead, approaching then fading away.

Mel leaned back and whispered, "I think we're alone now."

Janey giggled. Mel kissed her.

Mel's hand was on her breast, stroking the nipple hard through the layers of blouse and bra, the sweater pushed aside. She gasped as Mel's teeth nipped her lower lip gently; she plunged her tongue into Mel's mouth and felt her gasp in return. They kissed until her neck was stiff—*is that why they call it necking?* she thought foolishly—and Mel pushed her down gently onto the blanket.

Their mouths pressed together, Mel's tongue invading her, making her want to be fucked. Her breath came faster and faster until she felt lightheaded. Mel's fingers squeezed her breasts. With a shimmy and a sigh, Mel came to lie halfway on top of her, and her hand slipped underneath as Janey lifted herself to accommodate it. She felt the hook-and-eye clasp of her bra give way to her lover's practiced touch.

Mel's fingers were cool on her stomach, under the knit fabric of her blouse, coolly slipping under the gauzy inner lining of her bra cup. Her mouth was hot, sucking Janey's tongue into her own mouth, and Janey couldn't concentrate on both. She moaned deep in her throat, surrendering conscious thought, letting her body feel the soft-hard sand shift under them, the scratchy wool of the old blanket under her bare legs, skirt riding up of its own volition, Mel's muscular body pressed against her as her hand roved, the cool air on her now-naked midriff. Her skin was cool, but her pussy was on fire. She spread her legs, willing her lover's hand to delve between them.

Mel's chuckle rumbled in her chest. Her mouth still pressed to Janey's, she shifted until almost all her weight was on Janey, and Janey thought she might pass out from excitement alone, her breath coming hard, but not from the pressure of Mel's body. It was Janey who broke off the kiss.

"I want...I want...," she told her lover, not at all coherent.

Mel's hand pulled Janey's skirt up roughly and pushed her chino-clad knee between them. "What do you want, baby?" She rested on her elbows, and Janey looked up, trying to see her lover's face in the deepening shadow. Her eyes glinted, her pupils black pools. Mel's thigh that was pressed against her crotch, hard and hot and motionless, was maddening.

Janey shivered, too aroused to be embarrassed as usual, feeling like a teenager no matter how old she got. "I want you to fuck me."

Mel was breathing hard, too. She started to move, rocking her hips ever so slightly, and Janey groaned, rising to meet her.

"Don't you know," Mel panted, "that dry-humping is traditional in this place?" Her pelvis ground in a slow rhythm, unhurried, hypnotic. Janey groaned again, a sound of protest this time. She would die if Mel didn't fuck her. But Mel ignored her protest.

"The summer I was eleven, just before we moved away," Mel began, her voice rough, "I came here with my best friend, Cindy. Our parents gave us each a book of tickets for the rides, but we snuck away." She paused to lick her lips, never halting the slow grind of her thigh against Janey's soaked crotch. "We wanted to see what the teenagers were doing." Janey's eyes were closed, and she felt excitement building deep in her belly as she moved with her lover, ever so slowly, like gentle swells rocking a boat at anchor.

Mel reached up and took Janey's chin in her hand, grasping it firmly. "Pay attention." She waited until Janey was looking into her eyes.

"We hadn't figured out sex yet. We knew about penises but not erections." She resumed the rhythm of her hips, relentless but slow, so slow that Janey thought she might cry. "We took Barbie's and G.I. Joe's clothes off and put them together like scissors, but we knew that couldn't be right." She chuckled at the memory.

Mel's hips twitched. "Mmmmm," she groaned, deep in her throat, and a surge of arousal shot through Janey. *Her, too*, Janey thought incoherently, *her, too*. She would come soon...whether she wanted to or not.

Mel cleared her throat. "Cindy and I came under here to see if other kids were doing it." Janey reached up to touch her lover's face, and saw her frown in concentration. Mel kissed her palm and went on.

"We couldn't see anything, really. They were wearing

bathing suits. Boys lying on top of girls, kissing."

Janey could picture the tanned, half-naked young bodies, the boys in their swim trunks, the girls in bikinis. The lines of brilliant light cutting across them, like frozen strobes. Heat and the smell of suntan lotion.

"One girl had her knees up and the boy was lying between her legs, moving like this." Mel pumped her hips a little faster, a little harder, and Janey wrapped her leg around Mel's thigh, groaning, rubbing, no longer even thinking of keeping quiet. Mel caught one of Janey's fingers in her mouth and sucked it, making both of them rock their hips faster, Janey panting, until finally Mel let it fall from her lips. She grabbed Janey's hand and held it down above her head, holding herself very still until Janey followed her lead and lay quiet.

"I remember Cindy asking me if I wanted to pretend I was a boy. If I wanted to practice kissing."

Mel lowered her face to Janey's and kissed her, shyly, just lips at first, then harder, lips soft and wet and full, until finally her tongue slipped out to lick Janey's.

Janey gasped, "Did you do that?"

"We did." Their bodies were moving again; Janey didn't know which of them started first.

Mel's mouth was on hers once more, her tongue pushing through Janey's lips, invading her. Mel's tongue probed her mouth, danced with her tongue like the writhing teenage bodies in the cool sand, ground their lips together, sucking and nipping, while Janey rode Mel's thigh as hard as she could, her wet cunt finding friction in the soaked crotch of her own cotton panties against Mel's trouser leg, clinging to her lover with sweat. She was just conscious enough to remember the words *dry-humping,* and she laughed to herself before she came, bucking against Mel, tipping over into an orgasm like a roller coaster dropping down in its final, heart-stopping descent.

Gradually, her heart stopped pounding. She could feel Mel's heart beating through her T-shirt, strong and only a little faster. Mel never came that way. She roused herself to ask, "Then what?"

"Cindy stopped. She got scared and ran out, and I ran after her." Mel sighed. "After we moved, I never came back here. I never saw Cindy again." After a moment of silence, Janey felt Mel smile, her face pressed against her own. "Funny, though. I caught a glimpse of a guy's hard-on, as I ran out. A girl was giving him a hand job."

"Ewww," Janey said automatically, her own eleven-year-old self rising out of the past.

"Yeah," Mel said, grinning into the dimming light. "Ewww is right. But then, I knew how sex worked."

Janey pushed Mel off her, onto the blanket. It was almost completely dark now; when she looked out, down the beach, Janey could see the distant, reflected lights of the amusement pier scattered and dancing on the waves. She ran her hand down her lover's reclining body until she found her belt. She unbuckled it. Mel didn't stop her. The ghosts of calliope music, ancient lovers, and two curious girls broke up in the faint salt breeze and blew away.

Janey unbuttoned the fly and unzipped it, the heat of her lover's soft belly rising to her hand. She slipped her fingers under the elastic of Mel's briefs. Mel shifted, to let the pants open wider. Janey propped herself on her elbow and pushed through the crinkly hair of Mel's bush.

"I think," Janey said, sliding her fingers into the slippery wet folds of Mel's pussy, "that a hand job is also traditional in this place."

"I think," Mel echoed, gasping as Janey's thumb lit on the hard nub of her swollen clit, "you may be right."

Riding the Rails
Jack Perilous

Since hooking up with Mimi a few years ago and graduating
from the promiscuity of college, I've felt a bit *over* public sex.
As a dyke—a butch with a femme—I grew tired of the edge of
real fear that surrounds otherwise blissed-out public hookups.
Instead, I've discovered the joy of bedrooms where we and
our invited guests do exactly what we want, for as long as we
like, without the aid of concealing shrubbery.

We headed back to our Brooklyn apartment last Saturday
night via the 6 train, which doesn't actually go to Brooklyn.
You have to transfer to the 4/5 at the end of the line, and the
later it gets, the more screwed up the schedules. Finally we
reached the last station. "I'm tired," she murmured. "Let's
just sit here another minute."

I didn't think it was such a super idea, but her hair smelled
great on my shoulder. These new trains—sleek, silver, with
long benches instead of seats, and a blinking digital clock—
relax you. They make you feel surrounded by luxury.

"Last stop on this train," the loudspeaker repeated.
"Everybody off the train." BEEEEEP. Click. "Shit." We stared

onto the disappearing platform of the Brooklyn Bridge–City Hall station as the train, empty but for us, moved into a dark tunnel.

I wasn't sure where 6 trains go to sleep. Technically, New York City subways run all night, but that's not to say that *all* trains run twenty-four hours a day—not by a long shot. The train—locked, empty but for us, desolate, shiny—soon lurched to a stop, and she fell into me. "I'm scared," she moaned. Mimi—my blond, sexy, take-charge Mimi, who spends her days "assisting" some important older babe in midtown—is a fussy baby: cranky, adorable, refusing to be comforted.

"I know, sweetie." She leaned further into me, nestling her smooth, soft face in my neck, pressing her plump lips to my skin. Against my arm, her nipple grew erect.

I'm like a man seized by desire and by the desire for control. I was all over her, pushing her into the seat, unbuttoning the top two buttons of her shirt, kissing the sweet-smelling strip between her breasts, pulling her soft nipples into my mouth and rolling them between teeth and tongue until they got hard. She's so beautiful. I want her more all the time, and each time I see her, or make her come, it sets me to wanting her again. She leaned back against the smooth, hard seat, moaning, hair falling in a tangle behind her. I sucked a dark red spot to the skin of her neck, and found her wet, open mouth—so much like a cunt—with my own, while my hand pushed open her thighs.

The train didn't so much as lurch. We were trapped, locked in, and definitely alone. What the hell. I sat up, undid my necktie, pulled her body lengthwise on the seat as she smiled curiously up at me, and bound her soft hands to the guardrail that borders the long bench. She squirmed and smiled. Her face, when turned on, is even more lovely than usual—sweet, trusting, her eyes a bit spacey, her lips parted. I slipped my hand back between her legs, parted them, and found that wet cunt waiting for me. I love to fuck her tied up, out of control, her arms stretched above her head, her tits standing up, her trying to move—or pretending to try—but finding herself unable to. I'm the only person who's ever fucked her, and it's a source of endless arousal to touch this blissfully submissive girl where no one else has ever touched her. It's like taking her virginity over and over. Tying her up in an abandoned subway car in a dark subway tunnel, the site of so much fear for women, was the ultimate domination for us, the final reclamation of *our* space, funded by *our* tax dollars and obscenely high fares, for our own sicko purposes. "Slap me," she breathed, and I did, with my pussy hand. I pushed my wet fingers into her mouth, made her suck them, before I put them back between her legs.

The train jerked and slowly began to move.

I didn't untie her. Fear passed over her face. "Not until I let you come," I whispered, though I felt the way she looked. Trespassing is illegal. Is fucking? My dick throbbed. I found that cleaved spot that I can only feel when she's close, and circled it hard and fast, pulling her hood around her clit with the weight of my whole hand. "Oh, Jesus, let me come, please let me come," she whimpered as she wet my hand. "Please shoot inside me."

"Tell me how much you love my hard dick popping your cherry," I commanded. Mimi moaned and came hard, pussy clenching on my hand, nails digging into my arm, in three hard spasms, and I pulled my soaked hand from between her legs and scrambled to untie her wrists as the train moved slowly onto the uptown platform.

Lip Service
Rosalind Christine Lloyd

Desperation can drive you to do the most revealing things.

Fired abruptly from my last job because I wasn't virtuous enough to ignore the frequent passes my boss's sexy wife was liberally forcing on me, I was struggling and needed to make some cash. Fast. Eventually my brain kicked in, and she and I realized we had something special in common—an obsession with expensive French lingerie (obviously one of the reasons I was so broke). Furthermore, our mutual obsession led to another one: We both loved fucking beautiful women wearing expensive French lingerie while we ourselves wore the same. Now, it didn't matter that everyone knew my boss was cheating on his wife, sleeping with many of my stupid, immature coworkers. But it *did* matter when one of those same coworkers told him about his wife and me. So he fired my ass out of there, but kept his bitch, and I suppose on some level I'm lucky no one found my body floating in the East River.

So then not only was I broke, but my own small business was almost out of capital. I may have been out of luck for a time, but I was far from out of ideas, for I've always been a Jill of any trade. Notice I don't say *all* trade. But I'll try almost anything once, just as long as it doesn't compromise my feminine lesbian integrity too much.

My integrity got a good workout a few years ago with a woman called Feather Jackson. It was her vision, while just a sophomore in one of those super sister colleges in New England, to provide special services to women, and women only. She came up with the name Lip Service, and a business plan written on the back of a bar napkin.

I happened to be at the same bar at the time, and fell for her charms, big-time. I remember our first night like it was yesterday, me chin deep in Feather's oozing bush, thick with its wild honey sticking to me like an omen to a prophet. I had died and gone to heaven: Feather had that effect on me. I didn't care if we did anything else, I knew I needed to orally gratify this woman every single time I came near with her. She knew it too, and she loved it.

"Oh, Wish, my darling," she purred in the early morning, "if I cum anymore there won't be any more of me left. You give it like no one I've ever known." She gurgled an orgasm from her thick lips.

"You got it like that, Feather," I murmured, my tongue not missing a beat as I drove it deeper into her moistened, warm soft folds of labia-flesh. I felt flattered by her compliments but was far too busy to really care at the moment.

"Yes. The best. My darling you are the absolute very best," Feather moaned. Over and over and she growled, like a panther in heat, pushing herself into my face both tightly and forcefully. *Such sweet reward,* I remember thinking.

The real reason for the compliment? Well, Feather had a notorious reputation—not a bad one, just a persistent one. She had been, shall we say, *around* the campus many times over, enjoying the pick of the litter. Feather is that typically highly attractive woman gifted with the kind of frighteningly beguiling beauty one could not ignore. She was magnetic, and did she ever know it. No one could tie her down. Soon she could no longer fit me into her busy fuck schedule, and I began to miss seeing her. Eventually, I found out just how busy she was when rumors began surfacing that Feather would let you do things to her...let us say, sexual things...for a price. Tuition was going up, was her attitude; bills needed to be paid, and a girl had to eat!

Some years and an MBA later, Feather opened a more regular business, building on her legacy and calling it Lip Service. It was one of those private, not so typical escort agencies with a truly exclusive following. If I hadn't known any better I would have sworn she was turning me out to prepare me for a brief role in her own destiny. She became the envy of certain pockets of the community because not only did she achieve incredible success, financially speaking, but she took pleasure in the fact that she didn't have to promote "estrogen parties," or build a legitimate mailing list, or secure a liquor license, or come up with an obscene overhead—or, more importantly, pay any taxes.

Feather often told me, though I didn't see her often, that when I got tired of pursuing my dream (I design specialized fetish wear), she would always have a place for me "in the business."

One night, feeling depressed about my sorry state of affairs, I stepped into Lilith's, a high-profile women's lounge where one can avoid the riffraff and rub shoulders with an older, rustier, ritzier crowd of ladies. Lilith's had often helped me resist the temptation of overcomplicating my life with hungry, horny, short-term opportunists. So whom did I run into, looking splendid in a sophisticated, expertly fitted Italian suit and height-defying stilettos, but Ms. Feather herself.

"Hold on, girl," she said into her cell. "Wish Livingston! I know I'm seeing you for a reason," she declared, clutching a jeweled mobile phone in one hand, an apple martini in the other, while pinching a cigarette between her lips.

"Always in your business head, girl," I replied, batting away the smoke while kissing her on each cheek. Gazing at her, I thought, *I could sure use a facial, a manicure, a few shots of botox—a whole friggin' makeover.* Feather was groomed to the max.

"I'm not *always* about business, just most of the time," she murmured, giving me a little feel. "And look at you! Still looking scrumptious, Wish. Don't change."

Scrumptious? What was that about? "How's the business and you?" I asked instead.

"Both booming. Making money hand over fist. I'm here for a thirty-minute escape because there's never a break. I have no idea what a vacation is, darling. And I have two beautiful lovers who could–not–be–happier. So, I guess you can say life is good. Come, Wish. What are you drinking? Let me treat you to something nice. We need to wet our whistle a little. And enough about me. Tell me, you look like you lost your best friend."

"You're not too far from the truth."

"So tell me, what's the matter."

So I poured out my heart to her—or, more accurately, 'fessed up to all my personal financial and business woes— while now and then a few women greeted her at her barstool as if she were the fucking mayor.

"Darling," she said, when I ran out of sob story, "I am so sorry about your little clothing line. Small businesses can be tough at times. Let me think on that because I may be able to help you. But outside of that—you still look good, woman. What, you don't have some girlfriends around to give you some of that good old moral support?"

"Having a woman is the last thing on my mind. I'm trying to pay the rent, Feather."

"Of course. You were never one to let sex screw up your budget. Wish, you are too damn fine to be without a woman. I know you haven't lost your touch."

"Lose my touch? Never." Was she kidding? *Me?* Lose my touch? I only wish that other things in my life came to me as quickly and as easily as women. Still, my life was far from the ideal. Cheap prix fixe meals and happy hours couldn't repair that.

"This calls for a celebration," Feather declared, eyeing me up and down over and over while summoning Molly the bartender.

"A celebration?" said Molly. "And what are we celebrating?" The girl was at the ready with a chilled bottle of Dom along with two crystal flutes from a locked cabinet.

"We're celebrating a potential business deal," Feather said to the world at large, taking a long suck on her cigarette before raising her champagne glass, tipping it in my direction.

"Potential?"

"Yours is a wasted talent if you can't get paid for it, my dear! What you do, that thing you're good at, can be quite lucrative." Feather's eyes narrowed to a seductive squint as she slid down in her seat, licking her champagne-coated lips.

I was thinking, *Bitches couldn't pay me enough.* But who was I fooling? My rent was in arrears like a mutherfuck. I had interviewed for almost twenty legit jobs, but not one of them turned up an offer. Eating pussy for pay was probably the easiest thing in the world I could do to make some cash.

"Give me a week," Feather said, breaking into my reverie. "I can guarantee you at least a thousand bucks. That's right.... Two clients a day for three days total—only thirty minutes per job. It's that simple. If you can handle the pace, woman, you can make serious good money. I've got the clients. My problem is, I don't have enough good orals on staff."

Okay. So I cringed. Just a little. But fuck modesty. I love pussy. I love giving head and I know I'm great at it.

"All right, Feather. If you can promise me that kind of money for three days' work, maybe I'll give it a try."

"Wish. Once you try it, I know you're going to like it." Feather was smiling so jubilantly I could have sworn she was seeing dollar signs in my eyes.

"Now, ya' know this is high-class pussy we're talking here," she went on. "Ladies paying good money for our services. Young and old. Some are a joy to work with, others are bloody bitches. From the frustratingly frigid to the hot as hell. Extra wet to super dry."

"Give me something to look forward to, won't you," I pleaded.

Feather laughed with high drama and slammed her champagne flute down on the bar. "It's the reality of the business. There's always the good, the bad, and the ugly—you know, like college was for us. Either way, darling, it's all tax-free cash, and that's the most attractive thing of all."

So it was settled. I decided to give it a try for a week. I could hardly believe things had come to this...I was stooping to new lows. But if those dykes were willing to pay $300 for a lick-and-suck job, well—shit—why not?

Okay. So the week turned into three months, and I had to buy a new bag to hold all the cash.

Besides paying my rent in full and catching up on all my bills, I opened a savings account, started a 401(k), replaced my wardrobe with pretty and elegant things, gave my studio apartment an unbelievable makeover, and even developed a weekly schedule that included a personal trainer, manicures, pedicures, massages, high-colonics, and hair stylings—not to mention that I stocked a whole warehouse of vitamins and natural herbal remedies to keep me nice and strong and my disease resistance high. I never got sick. Not only had I become financially secure, but I felt beautiful. My reputation for giving an orgasm in just under fifteen minutes was spreading in the community. I was the #1 most requested of Feather's lot and could hardly keep up with the demand. Imagine that!

The details? Generally I use a very special chair to perform the deed. It's comfortable and it relieves the lesbian whiplash I suffer from—you know, occupational hazard. Unless of course I get a request to use a bed, dresser, or shower, or to stand up against a wall, or just free stand. I've also worked in public and private restrooms, in stairwells, on fire escapes, on desks in private offices, in cars and trucks, even on a motorcycle (parked, of course). I've also pulled some trains at a few bachelorette parties that paid me so much I could hardly believe it. Trust me, I'm on a total E spell when those incidents occur. I can hardly remember a thing. But now get this: After all this cunnilingus, I never–ever–come. Of course there have been those who have tried to get me to, in their own way, but alas, without success.

I was roaring along with back-to-back, belly-to-belly appointments. I had an impressive record in Feather's business, and I eventually was able to overlook the envy of catty coworkers. As for Feather, she was content to see her profits rise. Some eighty percent of my clients were return/repeat. I was familiar with practically everyone I "dated," so this made work easier— except for the one who "*discovered*" Lip Service one day. On my way to meet my personal trainer, I got a call on my cell.

"Wish. You have a request." I was a little surprised to hear Feather's voice on the other end of the phone, calling in a date.

"Oh yea? A regular?"

"No, honey."

"So, how do you know she's okay?" I was a bit miffed about missing my workout.

"She's a referral, girl. Don't be so suspicious. *I'm* calling this in."

"So just because you're calling it in, is that supposed to make me feel better?"

Feather had a way of making me feel like I shouldn't be suspicious about her business practices. She had to be just as apprehensive about this date as I was. Especially since Tammy, the scheduler, hadn't made the call to me herself.

Now this was not the type of business where walk-ins are encouraged, although I did them occasionally. But I didn't like it.

"Okay, Feather," I persisted when she remained silent. "What's up? Why *you* calling?"

"Girl, ain't nothin' suspicious about this. The chick called, she asked for you, she's a referral—apparently one of my high-profiled clients recommended you. I checked it out. She's clear. So take your pretty ass to 173 West 10th at two A.M. And don't be late this time. Everybody knows how good you are, but stop being so damn ornery about it, 'kay?"

And then the click of a disconnect. That fucking Feather. I had to go.

In three months I hadn't had a single "situation." That is, a problem with a date. Not that there was a rash of situations at Lips, but that didn't mean there weren't enough to keep us on our toes. I almost had a situation at a bachelorette party. I was working on this chick when the woman who was being honored started to finger me. Viciously. I'm talking some serious buttfucking here. Now, everybody's got rules. Mine are simple. When working, don't touch me. Particularly when a bunch of hungry butches are staring at my ass as if it were buried treasure. Well, the guests didn't like it one bit when I reminded them of the rule I had announced at the very beginning of the party. I didn't care how much more money they were offering, and believe me, a bunch of inebriated bulldaggers with Friday's paycheck burning holes in their bras starving for some pussy-for-hire can get wildly out of control. I'm not into giving *my* shit away. Luckily, I got myself out of that one, but I've heard stories where some of my coworkers weren't so lucky.

But I had to get down to 10th Street, so I convinced myself to stop overprocessing. I've had walk-ins before. But deep down I felt that this one would turn out to be a bit odd. It was just my gut talking, and it never lies.

Luckily, I had squeezed in a wax, a manicure, and a pedicure one day earlier, so I felt hot to trot. I dressed in my favorite work dress, a slinky red wrap-around, with not a stitch on underneath—I like to show my stuff—and a pair of too-sexy Manolos finished with my vintage Burberry trench.

I had a double shot of Makers Mark before catching a taxi to the West Village. One's mind can never be ready for every eventuality, but at least I was relaxed and at some ease. Little did I know that nothing would prepare me for what was to come.

When I arrived, I was in my business-as-usual head. I was a working girl. Ringing the doorbell for the third time, I thought, *Hmm, this could be a potential situation.* I was turning away when the buzzer whizzed me in with a sharp staccato. I pushed the front door open, hesitating to rush through it. Checking my watch, I knew I was only five minutes late. I'm never early for anything. It was a normal enough New York City apartment building, nothing particularly glamorous, though the neighborhood was far from funky-cheap. The second floor was an easy enough climb. Taking two steps at a time I exhaled at the flash of cool air that sneaked between my legs underneath my dress.

"It's open," a nice enough voice called from inside the apartment.

I walked into a modest-sized room. Nothing struck my eye

in the Pottery Barn-esque décor. The place was clean, tastefully decorated. Maybe too clean. Before I could make up my mind, a woman appeared. She was as average looking as her apartment, with long black braids going down her back. Her skin was a nice even tone, the color reminding me of how I take my coffee. Average height, average weight. She wore a long, black silk robe. Not a bad-looking woman at all, but not striking. Like, you might offer to buy her a drink at last call without feeling bad about it.

"So, you're Tasha," she said, hands folded across her chest, examining me closely. Tasha was my working name. I liked using it.

"Yeah. And you must be…?" I asked, peeling my coat from my shoulders and laying it across the sofa, shaking my dreads so they lay neatly against my back.

"I'm Eden. A very good friend of mine recommended you. Hmm, she was right about how beautiful you are."

I'm not one for small talk during these things. I work by the clock. Date-protocol while working did absolutely nothing for me.

"Thanks, Eden. So, you wanna get started?" I was already in front of her, wrapping my arms around her torso. I felt her stiffen in my embrace.

Stepping back away from me, she said, "Uhm, Tasha. Can you relax for just a moment? Give me a second to absorb this, please. I don't warm up as quickly as you, given these conditions."

"Fine. We can get the business part out of the way first, then. Just so you're aware, it's two-fifteen. We're on the clock. It's three hundred for the first half hour. Go over the first half hour, it's fifty dollars every ten minutes after that, or a hundred and fifty for the second half hour. You can pay me now. Are we clear?"

Eden went to her wallet, pulling out twenties. "Listen,

Tasha. I've never paid for sex before. So this is a little awkward for me."

"Okay. Do you drink?" I asked, counting the money she handed me before placing it in a hidden pocket inside my trench coat.

"Occasionally."

"Do you have anything to drink here?"

"Some scotch."

She gestured to a trim little wet bar in the corner, and I poured two drinks. I had to break the paper label on the bottle. "Drink this," I told her, handing her a glass while sipping my own.

She accepted the drink, sniffing it cautiously, saying, "I hope this helps, because I hate the taste of hard liquor."

After a long swallow I replied, "Once you get over the initial shock on the tongue, the rest gets real easy. Trust me. Now take a nice sip." *Because I don't plan to stay here all night...unless you're paying.*

She took a quick sip, her face caving into a pretty grimace before she drained the glass. I walked over to her entertainment center and cruised her CD collection, finally deciding on Me'shell Ngedeocello. She has a way of making women feel vulnerable, sexy, and easy to fuck—and this was what I was going for. I find Wagner has the same effect.

So I turned around and Eden was just standing there, staring at me. I checked the clock. If we were gonna waste time, it'd be on her own goddam Benjamin Franklins. I suggested she sit down on the sofa, because my quickie sensual massage always got results in the relaxation area.

Many women require, and demand, foreplay. Technique, I tell everybody, is everything. In my line of work, you don't want to spend a lot of time on foreplay, as it's quite easy for the receiver to linger in the moment till, when the time's up, she suddenly doesn't want to pay for more. It can become problematic. Sometimes I just want to get in and get out. So I invited Eden to get undressed and to sit. At first she was shy. I told her to take her time, as I checked my watch and lit a cigarette. After a brief hesitation she slipped out of her robe, letting it fall to her feet so that I could get a good look at her. She had a good body—not perfect, no centerfold possibility here. She looked wholesome and well fed, with nice breasts the size of honeydews, with perky, nice nipples. Her upper torso balanced nicely with really curvaceous hips. She was thicker than what superficial gals would consider an average size, but I thought she was just fine. I smiled at her, to indicate that everything was okay, and with a subtle motion of my free hand invited her to sit. When she sat, I took a drag, blew a smoke ring, and unwrapped my dress from around my body, presenting her with my naked and very expensive self. I posed, hands on my hips, legs spread apart. My no-nonsense stare may have been too direct for her, but I needed to present the merchandise in a positive fashion. She seemed to approve, finally smiling.

Putting out the cigarette, I stepped behind her and began an intense, deep tissue massage on her shoulders and back. This took her to another place as her body began responding to my touch, her anxiety dissolving in my hands. Her breathing slowed, shifting deep down in her chest, becoming a divine moan as I dug deeper into her tight flesh. This was where I wanted her. I allowed my hands to roam down her back and around her shoulders to her soft and heavy breasts. Balancing them in the palms of my hands, I raised them slightly before pushing them together, caressing them tenderly. Kneading her honeydew breasts gently from underneath I cradled her nipples between my thumbs and index fingers, squeezing them gently, for a few seconds applying some pressure and not letting go. Her breathing began to quicken as I felt the temperature of her skin increase. Good. She was warm and ready for this experience. Many of my dates were not this easy.

After running my hands all over her body, I took note that twenty minutes had gone by since I walked through her door. But I was kind enough not to want to leave her undone. I walked from behind the sofa to face her. Her eyes were closed tight, and she trembled a little, as if anticipating what was to come. As I was about to kneel down between her legs, her eyes popped open and she said, "That massage was wonderful. Would you mind doing it some more, just for another ten minutes?" I was struck. My massage was not all that spectacular. But hey, she was paying.

"Okay. Sure. But I want to remind you, Eden that—"

"I know. I know. I've paid you for the half hour. There's more where that came from if—" (her once innocent eyes narrowed on me with a wicked glint) "—if there's more where *that* came from?"

Now if I hadn't known any better I would have sworn that Eden thrust her jaw out as if motioning toward my crotch. *My* crotch! Like she was getting some! I laughed out loud, knowing this little scene was going to be over sooner rather than later. The important thing was not to let the date have the upper hand—not even the illusion of it.

"Business first," I murmured. "You want another massage, you're gonna have to kick in for another half hour because I'm not in this for the massage and this will obviously go over." That moment right then was how you made money. I posed, did a smart French inhale, and flexed the muscles in my Pilates-toned thighs.

Eden looked at me. I couldn't know what she was thinking, but I guessed she was irritated. What was the hesitation? Why not? This was Grade A, one hundred percent pure chocolate-fied thunder right in front of her. I was worth that, and more. And I was calling the motherfuckin' shots.

Eden got up and disappeared into her bedroom, returning

with fourteen crisp Andrew Jacksons and four Abe Lincolns, as if she had just printed them herself. She walked so close to me that I could smell her all hot and moist as she laid the bills down next to my purse before returning to the sofa. Taking one last deep exhale before walking behind her, I started once again with the requested massage.

Before I knew it, Eden's arms flew up over me in one swift movement, flipping me over her head, forcing me to bury my face in her overgrown sweet, pungent bush, then her own juicy lips began gnawing at my naked cunt.

Pilates and my self-defense classes could not have prepared me for the powerful Ms. Eden. She was at least forty pounds heavier than me, and it was all sheer muscle. My legs kicked for a short time as I tried to avoid letting her mouth near my cunt, fighting like mad to push myself off her. But the strangest thing happened. As I fought that strong woman, her mouth performed the most heavenly magic on me that I had ever experienced in my whole damn life. And as I continued to fight, her thick, soft, skillful tongue did things I never thought possible. The harder I fought, the more luscious she felt between my legs, between my swelling lips, right on my clit. Her arms were strong enough that she could hold my whole body off the floor and rub me against her, up and down, slow and steady, her arms wrapped so tight around me I knew I would be bruised, her fingers firmly gripping my limbs while she moved me around against her mouth and tongue like a naked rag doll. My own arousal betrayed me as I became hot liquid against her, my thighs quivering, my sex moving to the rhythm that she created.

I came quickly, with a shout of surprise. And then I stole a glance at my watch: damned if there wasn't still time on the old clock.

Gently she lowered me right side up onto her lap, allowing me to disengage from her muscular, sweaty vise-like grip.

Wait, I was pissed! Violation, any violation of the rules, was not cute, as far as I was concerned, no matter how cute the date. And she wasn't my type. At all. But it was obviously a done deal.

Speechless and angry, I walked over to my clothing and began to dress. Eden followed, pressing her index and middle finger between her sated lips to indicate that she wanted a cigarette. After wrapping my dress around my body and tying it, I pulled a smoke from my case and tossed it on her desk before snatching the cash, my purse, and my coat, then hastily headed for the door.

"Why so bitter?" Eden shouted at my retreating back. "*You're* the one that had the orgasm. Not me. And keep the change, sweetie—that's your tip." I slammed the door shut behind me.

Needless to say, that little experience signaled the end of my career at Lip Service. There was no excuse any longer for continuing to sell "it," because the money I had made more than caught me up on my bills and helped my own business get back on its feet. Obviously, all along, it had been the one-way sex that made me stay. Clients who violated my...well, my *parameters*...were not my thing. Feather understood that. In fact, I later discovered that Eden was one of Feather's very happy lovers. Damn. I should have known better.

Alice and the Red Queen
Jean Roberta

Alice liked the roar of the power mower and the smell of freshly cut grass. The trickle of sweat beneath her breasts and the pull in her bare arms and thighs made her feel like a real dyke, like the great tennis player who had hired her to groom her immense back lawn. Alice tried to ignore the throbbing of the motor as she wondered if she should consider a career as a landscape gardener.

Felicity Pakingham stood on her deck, gin-and-tonic in hand, watching the college student in shorts and halter top who rode her mower up and down the lawn, dividing it into neat sections. Felicity could see Alice's breasts bouncing from meters—or yards—away.

Squinting toward the sun, Alice was dazzled by the copper-colored beacon of Felicity's very short hair. Ten years before, a British sports reporter had named her "The Red Queen" after a merciless ruler in a fantasy chess game that had preceded all the currently popular computer games by over a century. The name had inspired cartoon portraits of Felicity, including a computerized image of a tennis-playing queen. None of these caricatures did justice to the real woman's bold-featured beauty.

Felicity knew that she was slightly past her prime as an athlete, but her muscles were still sleek and hard. She could see that Alice was not used to sustained physical effort, although she could tolerate discomfort. The girl's pampered young curves and her determination both tickled Felicity, who smiled down as though at a worthy opponent. The prospect of an interesting game made her aware of her hands as well as her clit.

As she took a sip of her drink, she saw Alice look up toward her. Then, despite the rosy cheeks brought on by her work, she clearly began to blush on being stared at.

"Would you like to take a break?" called Felicity in a voice full of cheer, but with an insinuating undertone. "You must be thirsty. A cold drink will revive you." Alice almost fell off the mower in gratitude.

Climbing the wooden steps to the deck, Alice touched the cotton scrunchy that held her chestnut hair in a ponytail to keep it off her face. Even still, sweaty tendrils had to be pushed away from her forehead. She wondered if her movements looked awkward to the Red Queen, whose body language had always been elegantly direct, both on and off the court.

"I have gin, scotch, beer, and lemonade," offered Felicity, playing the hostess. "You may have whichever you like, but alcohol will make you feel hotter when you get back to work."

Alice couldn't look into the sparkling blue eyes of her idol. "Then I'd like lemonade, please," she answered demurely.

"You're a good girl, aren't you, dear?" purred Felicity, almost laughing openly. "Come into the kitchen. I'll get your lemonade from the fridge."

Standing in the cool, gleaming shade of Felicity's kitchen,

Alice regarded the offered glass bottle as a welcome distraction. Felicity held the girl's outstretched hand in both of hers for a moment, and her touch felt electric to Alice. "You want to do a good job, don't you?" the Red Queen demanded.

"Yes." Alice gulped from the bottle as though her drink could make her articulate or competent, preferably both. "Of course."

Felicity ran a firm hand down Alice's drinking arm, making her shake. "What did you tell me you are studying?" she teased. "Not landscape gardening, is it? Pity that sort of thing isn't your forte."

Alice felt devastated, even though she knew that the Red Queen wasn't completely serious. "Am I doing something wrong?" begged the girl, forcing herself to look at Felicity's face. Alice knew that her large brown eyes must look hopelessly naïve, but she couldn't pretend that working for a celebrity didn't make her very nervous.

"Alice," Felicity addressed her as though speaking to a young child. "Come look." With a thrilling hand on the small of the girl's back, Felicity guided her onto the deck to survey her own work. "I appreciate that you're not finished yet," the Red Queen explained patiently. "But look at the borders of the lawn. The grass hasn't been evenly mowed, so you'll have to use something else to finish the edges. You weren't planning to do that, were you?"

Alice took in the lush expanse of grass and flowers. She didn't think the mowed area looked bad compared to her parents' lawn: the yard on which she had cut her mowing teeth, so to speak. But she knew she hadn't done a job worthy of a queen's castle grounds.

"My garden is my refuge," sighed Felicity, as if to herself. "I want it to be well-ordered, peaceful, soigné, private, and discreet. Like a trusted companion." Her hand slid shockingly from Alice's back to squeeze one of her buttcheeks and linger there, as if claiming the territory. Here it was: a lucky girl's wildest dream about to come true. Yet it wasn't happening in the way she had dreamed it.

"I'm sorry," Alice groaned. She shifted her stance, still tingling under Felicity's hand. "Ma'am. I'll even up the edges. I'll do whatever you want." She took a deep breath, determined to speak her mind. "I know I'm not a professional gardener. I never told you I was. If that's what you really wanted, you wouldn't have hired me."

"Cheeky," remarked Felicity, who looked amused. She punctuated the remark with a light slap to Alice's behind.

The girl closed her eyes to break the Red Queen's spell, and awkwardly moved away from her. "No," retorted Alice, fighting off tears. "No. I'm not. Ms. Pakingham, I admire you more than I can say, and I would be glad to take care of your garden all summer, for nothing. But you have no right to blame me for not being an expert. You knew I wasn't a professional gardener or a tennis champion. I'm trying, but I wasn't born knowing everything that's important to you. I know other things. I've won scholarships in math, which is my major. I can beat you at the video game that was named after you. And I'll still have a life after you've forgotten me."

Felicity felt touched. Alice's anguish seemed heartfelt, even though she couldn't possibly imagine how Felicity herself, whose victories had been cheered by millions, could fear being forgotten while she was still alive.

"Ah," breathed the Red Queen. "You don't want to be patronized." She smiled and pulled Alice into her arms, bringing her enormous relief. Alice felt as if she could come from being held this way.

Alice couldn't believe it when Felicity touched her mouth to her own. Its demanding warmth made Alice feel as if her bones were melting. Her grateful moan encouraged Felicity to part the girl's lips with her own gin-flavored tongue and slide it into her mouth, making Alice abandon her lemonade for sweeter pleasures.

Felicity withdrew to let the girl catch her breath, but she pressed her crotch against Alice's belly and hip, letting her feel the hard object that Felicity wore under her capri pants. The Red Queen held Alice's eyes with her own. "You are a lesbian, aren't you, my dear?" she drawled.

"Oh yes," grinned Alice. "I love—women."

"Would you ride a cock horse to Banbury Cross?" teased Felicity.

"There and back."

"Tell me something, Alice," cooed Felicity. "Answer honestly. If I'm not satisfied with your work, would you prefer to know that you'll never be invited here again, or would you accept a penalty, so that you could earn a second chance?"

Alice knew in her awakened clit, in her expectant bottom, and in her swollen nipples what was coming. Nonetheless she asked, "What's the penalty?"

"A spanking," promised the Red Queen, slipping her fingers under Alice's shorts. "On your bare arse, over my knee. I won't patronize you by underestimating your endurance, my girl. Smart strokes shall show you the error of your ways. No quarter asked, and none given. You won't want to sit down for a week after."

Alice knew that she should feel alarmed and insulted, but she couldn't help grinning or squirming. She wondered if she could actually come from the impact of Felicity's strong hand on her tender skin, or feel a returning gush of pleasure and pride while studying the damage with the help of two mirrors in the privacy of her bedroom. Peering down the dark rabbit-hole of her own perversity made Alice feel faint.

Felicity gave her girl's impatient young buttcheeks a sharp pinch apiece. "You've made your choice, haven't you, my girl?" she prompted.

"Yes," admitted Alice. "Ma'am." She didn't know what else to say.

"Then finish your work and do it well. Or you might not get a chance to redeem yourself."

The sun offered no mercy to Alice, but she was determined not to overlook a single, uncouth blade of grass. Suffering from heat of various kinds, the girl still had her pride. After she had ridden over the entire lawn, she took the mower to the toolshed and picked out a hand-held tool for trimming the edges. By the time Alice finished, the lawn was ready even for a photo shoot.

She walked toward the deck, swaggering a little, as the other woman came toward her. "Beautiful," smiled Felicity. She was describing not only her garden.

"Anything for you," bragged the girl as the Red Queen held her glowing face in both hands and leaned forward to kiss her. Alice tasted her own salt on Felicity's mouth, and heard her own heartbeat.

Felicity drew back. "Anything?" she challenged, looking predatory. "We'll see." She enfolded the girl in her arms and found the knot at the back of her neck that held her halter-top in place. She soon had it untied, and pulled the yellow top down to reveal plump, pink breasts. The girl's nipples were already hard and red.

"Here?" asked Alice, glancing at the high wooden fence that couldn't guarantee protection from exposure.

"Where else?" smirked Felicity. "My sexy groundskeeper. This seems like the natural place for your ravishment." She rolled one of Alice's nipples between two fingers, squeezing it increasingly harder as the girl's breathing shook her rib cage. Before Alice could guess the next move, Felicity took the other nipple between her teeth and tormented it with her tongue.

The setting sun was streaking the sky lavender, pink, and gold. Playful breezes stroked Alice's bare skin as Felicity unzipped her shorts and pulled them down. The dark hair between the girl's pale thighs was matted with juice. Felicity smiled as the unmistakable smell floated to her nose. Slipping two fingers into the wet heat, Felicity collected Alice's nectar for tasting. "Ohh," moaned the girl. "Make me yours."

"Really?" sneered the Red Queen. "Are you giving me an order? How presumptuous. What a greedy wench you are."

"Or leave me alone," parried Alice, standing proudly naked in the summer twilight like a nymph in an old painting. She had set her hair free, and it flowed over her tanned shoulders. "If I'm not good enough, tell me to leave. I'll never come back. You can pretend you never met me."

Felicity nodded curtly, in an almost military gesture of respect. She couldn't keep the smile off her face. "I'm greedy too. I want your mouth, my dear." The Red Queen efficiently shucked her clothes and her favorite strap-on cock, leaving them strewn over the grass.

Alice knelt and paid homage to her idol's ginger-colored bush with careful hands and a daring tongue. The girl was more confident and experienced than Felicity had expected, and she soon discovered how to make Felicity groan and buck. Alice's face was wet when she raised it again.

"You have talent, girl," Felicity said. "You were meant to give pleasure. I want to know how much you can take. Like this...like the little animal you are." Felicity positioned her on all fours on the short, prickly lawn. "I have nothing to tie you with. Will you stay in place until I release you?" Alice nodded and did, and even spread her legs apart without being told.

The girl wiggled her bottom slightly while Felicity retrieved her valued tool and girded her loins. "This is what you want, isn't it?" she snickered, kneeling behind the girl and opening her wet cunt with one hand while holding her silicone cock with the other. She teased Alice with the head until the girl couldn't resist pushing back, wanting to be filled. With a well-placed lunge, Felicity sank it in to the hilt.

"Oh, Ma'am!" Alice burst out in an agony of pleasure. "Ohhh!" She had more to say, but Felicity's catchy rhythm silenced her for several beats. The girl knew from experience that the ecstasy of surrender, the sweetness of feeling completely owned, wouldn't last. As she grew impossibly wet, drenched by the storm in her eager young center, she wished she could record the experience and play it over and over whenever she needed to remember her brush with fame and power.

"It's—what we both want," the girl panted, squeezing the object that seemed amazingly realistic. "You too. Say it. Please. Say it."

Holding Alice by the hips, pressing against her warm behind, Felicity felt blessed. She felt a transfusion of something like innocence or like hope from this girl who gave herself so willingly without giving herself up. Felicity fucked her roughly, knowing that anything less would seem insulting.

"I want you," growled the Red Queen. "Want you! Won't—let you—go." She felt a subtle change deep inside her girl.

The wild ride ended too soon for both. Alice's climax felt like fireworks for an Amazon national holiday, while Felicity's was milder, being partly vicarious.

The two naked women sat entwined, watching the stars come out. "A video game might be named after you someday," mused the Red Queen, playing with Alice's breasts. "But you'll never rise too high for me to spank."

Alice felt a pang of despair, and wondered how she could ever have expected better treatment. "To keep me in my place? To remind me that I'm nobody in your world?" Her voice dripped with the sarcasm of disillusioned youth.

"Those intentions are hardly the same, sweet Alice," lectured Felicity, stroking her girl's tangled hair. Felicity sighed discreetly. "But certainly, you need to learn your place in my life. My meaning will sink in, I hope." And before long, it did.

Years later, a rumor surfaced in the tabloid press that Felicity Pakingham, having lost her edge, had plunged into a senseless affair with a young computer geek named Alice Liddell, a lesbian barfly with whom she had nothing in common. Felicity refused to dignify such gossip with a response, while Alice patiently explained to the nosy that she had formerly worked for Ms. Pakingham, nothing more. And she always seemed completely credible.

A Perfect Fit
Toni Amato

We work damned hard, my girl and I. Almost as hard as we play. It was August, and summer was at its hottest. We hadn't yet taken a vacation, so by the time we pulled out of the Alamo lot, we were more than ready for a little time just to ourselves. We're still as hot for each other as we ever were, back in those days of no-sleep-no-food-why-bother-with-clothes, but grown-up life is hard on sex and we're lucky to get time for a quickie here and there during the week. Like Queen Latifah says, "You've got things to do, but I have got things too, so I'll catch you on the weekend."

We had an entire week ahead of us, at a camp with like-minded folks who enjoyed a good fuck. "Adult Camp," they called it in the brochure, and when my girl and I read it through, there was no doubt in our minds that we were going to spend our vacation there. Grass and sun and, all day long, chances to have a little nookie. When you live in the city, your sex gets pretty contained. Thin walls. Housemates. Neighbors.

The car was packed with our supplies, and the year's com-pacted lust took up whatever space was left. I could barely keep my hands off my girl's ample belly as she drove. My sweet, juicy little fat girl. That's right. I'm a skinny guy, but I'm from the school of hot-and-a-lot; no pretty little plate with nothing on it but a lima bean, a carrot curl, and some neon sauce. I want my baby back-ribs. And my girl, when you've got your hands on her, you know you're getting you some one hundred percent U.S. D.yke A.pproved Choice.

I love being in the car with her. I love sitting across from her while she's concentrating on the road, and getting to look at her all I want, touch her all I want. Her ass is beautifully round and plump. She's got nice soft pillows of fat on her hips. Her thighs meet seductively, and I know what it's like to rest my head there. And then there's her belly. Don't get me started. The guys who go for the little skinny gals, they just don't know what a big, round, pouting belly can do, or the swelling breasts resting on it. I watched the way her belly pressed up against the steering wheel and rested on her broad thighs. She easily filled the driver's side of the sporty coupe we'd rented.

Me, I can't ever drive us anywhere. We'd be off the road and in a ditch in minutes. Which didn't seem like such a bad idea. It wasn't hot enough to have on a tank top, but her collar lay open wide enough to give me a great view of her ample, rounded cleavage. I grasped the dashboard and leaned closer, wishing I could fill my hands with her soft folds instead of cheap plastic and vinyl. I was just considering how much misbehavior I could get away with, maybe a hand on her inner thigh, maybe a quick brush across her breasts, when she let out a sigh.

"Dammit, we have to pull over."

"OK, baby. I was just thinking that very same thing."

Now normally, my randy guy routine gets me a playful slap, a raised eyebrow, and all the goodies that come afterward. This time all I got was the eyebrow.

"No. I mean we need to go back to Alamo."

We'd already been on the road for a good half hour and I know my girl hates to waste time, so this statement confused all hell out of me. Not to mention, it wasn't exactly the flirtation I was hoping for.

"This seat belt is cutting into me. I can't drive six hours like this." There were tears in her voice, mixed with rage. "Why can't they make these damn things so that they fit?" This wasn't the first time my girl had fallen victim to poor design. Movie seats. Airplane seats. Car safety belts. It's like the fashion magazines and retail clothing stores: Fat girls don't exist. And if they do, they should stay home. Naked.

Which I sort of agree with. Only not the same way. This kind of bullshit has ruined more than one hot date, and right then and there, watching my girl's face flush and hearing her voice shake, not from my powers of seduction, but from yet another ill-fitting thing, I made up my mind to fix this problem once and for all. At least for her.

"OK, baby. Turn around. We'll go right back there and get this taken care of. But pull over at the next rest stop first."

When a fat girl is reminded that the rest of the world thinks she's a monstrosity, let's just say her patience and good humor don't take it very well. My girl is a brave and courageous woman, but I could see tears forming in her eyes as she tugged at the last few inches of the seatbelt, which still cut cruelly into some of my favorite soft places.

"Why?"

I turned in my seat so that I was facing her, slid one arm slowly around the back of her neck and the other smoothly and gently under the warm fold of her belly. The weight of it on my forearm reminded me of how badly I wanted to put something else there.

"Because, Baby, if we have to return this car so soon, I think we really ought to take it for a ride, first."

She got my meaning, and despite the hurt and the frustration and the discomfort, that wicked, toothy bad-girl grin I love so much stretched across her face. Her thighs shifted a little and one hand moved from the steering wheel to my leg.

"Hmmm. I think I know of a good rest area just a few miles ahead."

I knew which one she was talking about, the State Line Lookout on the Palisades Parkway. Not a short drive at all, really. And God knows how far from the next Alamo, but the gleam in her eye let me know I had just offered her something much, much better than even all-you-can-eat night at the Country Buffet.

The parking lot is long and wide and the little stone restaurant never seems to be open. She chose a spot far away from the building where the streetlight's shine dappled through thick leaves, shut down the engine, and turned to me.

"Help me out of this thing."

She didn't have to ask twice. The red button at her side was an easy target and as I eased the seatbelt up and away, I slid my other hand under her shirt. I nuzzled her neck as I began to gently rub her belly, caressing away the creases and insults. A look of animal contentment filled her eyes as I slowly unbuttoned her flowered shirt, exposing sweet ample breasts tightly encased in an orange satin bra. I lifted and squeezed her bare, protruding belly, and she leaned back against the seat with a moan, and then pushed the seat adjustment lever back to the reclining position. My girl, she's darn clear about what she wants.

"These need to be set free," I said, unsnapping the front enclosure of her bra. Her 44DDs spilled into my palms, filling my hands with sweet warm flesh. I love the weight of my girl's breasts—at last, enough for a boy who's been hungry for years.

I slid the straps down her lush arms, and then tossed the bra to the floor. I cupped her large exposed breasts in my hands, then tenderly massaged each one until she moaned quietly.

"There, isn't that better? You look so sexy now, I want to fuck you right here, right now. Let's do it right here, and then give them their damn car back."

She arched her back slightly so her belly lifted. My fingers traced deep underneath all along where her flesh folds over, and my fingers sank into her softness.

"Yes, yes, yes," she said softly. Her hand on my thigh moved in small, firm circles. She pulled down my zipper, and then shifted her weight so that our bodies were more firmly pressed against each other. Feeling the warm, pliable flesh of her gut against my cock, I let out a groan of appreciation.

My head was pillowed between each splendid breast as my body curled around her giant belly and my hips thrust against her. I love to fuck her belly almost as much as I love to fuck her ass. Warm and heavy and moist. She ran her fingers through the short hairs at the back of my neck, then grabbed a fistful and yanked.

"Slow down, big boy. You've got a lot more work to do."

She slid her hands, palms down, under the elastic waist of her slacks and silky underwear, pushing them past her generous hips and down to her feet. Who says fat girls aren't limber? They just have to have a good enough reason to bother.

Her sharp, musky scent filled the car. I wanted to taste her, to bury my face deep between her luscious thighs and worship her plump mound until she begged me to stop. I ran my hands up and down, from her ears and neck down over her bosom and around and down her sides. Every time and every place, my hands reached something full and soft and open to my touch.

"You are the sexiest girl. Your breasts make my hands shake. Your belly drives me crazy. I want you, girl, so bad." I touched every part of her, especially the parts that were most soft, most pliable, most round, and that carried the most weight. I placed my hand against the softest part of her waist, where her skin gently starts forming a convex shape away from her chest. I love this soft, vulnerable spot.

Pulling away just far enough to climb over and on top of her, I reached quickly into the glove compartment and pulled out a condom I had put there earlier. Hope springs eternal and a Boy Scout is always prepared. She laughed, grabbed my cock, and slid the rubber on in one expert move.

"Show me what you were planning on doing, handsome."

The more I pressed into her, the more her whole body seemed to melt against me. Her lips opened, welcoming my tongue as she nipped and bit. Her arms circled my neck and drew me in close to her breasts. Her thighs spread slowly, opening little by little as I pushed into her, kissing and thrusting my tongue. I pushed myself against her rhythmically in that soft darkness, enveloped by her breast and belly and thighs.

I held her hips tightly, thrusting gently into her softness, rocking and swaying. I looked at this large soft woman beneath me, surrounding me. She wrapped her legs around my waist, and pulled me in deeper as she shook and shuttered. Her entire body rolled and rippled as I lay there and rode the waves until she relaxed and smiled up at me.

"I like the way we fit," she said.

Eighteen
Diane Thibault

August

She lifts her skirt for me. It's a plaid green and red skirt, with red lines, very fine, which she is wearing tucked under the bottom of a crisp white short-sleeve shirt, adorned with a thin green tie, loosened. Her shirt is unbuttoned, just enough for me to glimpse her succulent cleavage, bursting forth. Her brownness jumps out at me, makes her skin look smoother. She lifts up her skirt, grabs my hair, and pulls my head in, toward her cunt, exactly where she wants me to lick her, to make her come. I start, unable to resist her, her moans rising up and down, her juices trickling down my throat, until she explodes, faster than usual.

I look up. She is smiling, that mischievous smile that enslaved me, three months ago, when I first laid eyes on her. I know she's in a hurry, and she gives me a passionate but quick kiss before she heads out the door, running back to school after taking an overextended lunch break with me.

She is eighteen. I can't say that I'm in love with her, really, but I am certainly hooked on her, her charms, her body and its demanding nature, her stubbornness, the way she takes charge of our sexual encounters. She has allowed me to dominate her only once or twice. And hinted that she wants more, one day. Thinking of fucking her while she's tied up to my bed, slamming my dick inside her until she screams for me to stop, is the single most arousing thought I have ever had. My cunt throbs in achy anticipation even as I write this.

Once, a couple of weeks ago, she did let me fuck her, or rather, made me beg and kneel for her, then imperiously demanded that I fuck her right then and there, against the back of my couch, now stained with the contents of her pleasure. Even then, she didn't give an inch, even as I was fucking her mercilessly. The more I pounded into her, the more she possessed me, relished her power over me, the "older" woman she drives crazy, every time.

Sometimes I feel like a much older *man,* a suitor who guiltily and shamelessly showers my beloved with treasures untold, which only money and power can buy, knowing with a certainty that she will leave him one day, soon. That it is she who is in control—her youth being her only weapon.

One day out on the street with her, her legs still wobbly from a long, hard fuck, her by my side defiantly not holding my hand, instead admiring the bevy of young women on the steps of the café next door, we run into a friend of mine, who silently shames me with her disapproving stare then continues down the sidewalk.

But my friend does not understand, cannot know how delicious it felt when she seduced me, the first time I brought her back to my place. Touching me, touching me there, pressing her cool lips on mine, slipping her hungry tongue inside my mouth, while I inhaled her natural smell, a kind of subtle, flowery aroma. She knew she had me, right there and then. So she was never shy about touching me, taking me—in the washrooms of bars, at the movies, in the middle of the dance floor.

September

At her parents' home in the suburbs. One hot afternoon, after a rain shower. She is quite sure the house is empty. Puts on "Like a Virgin." Dances for me. I feel my blood rising, rising. She makes me hard.

She is slightly drunk. I, cold sober. She closes the blinds, locks her bedroom door, shoots a look at me, hungry.

Soon, we are rolling on the floor. Like dogs. Desperately yearning to connect, or else fight to the death trying.

She makes sure I'm on my back, holds my wrists down, takes off her pants, then panties. Silently, with a barely perceptible acceleration of breath, she brings her cunt to my face. Starving, I lick her, again and again. I also fuck her with my tongue, as she moans and grinds into me.

Immediately after she comes, she slides down, sitting on my stomach. Both of us catching our breath. She smiles. We know we'll never see each other again. This is strangely comforting.

She reaches over for a joint, lights it. Beads of sweat all over me. Her fresh kiss on my cheek.

The West Virginia Tattoo
Tennessee Jones

I love to fuck because I've been separated from the mountains. In the canyon streets of New York City I am rangy like a mountain lion, the smog and sky and shimmering, disappearing buildings like water falling senseless and white and soaking into hidden carpets of green moss. The silver sparkle of it blurs my vision sometimes, so that I imagine I am standing in the bed of the Colorado River inexplicably sucked dry, waiting for all that displaced and angry water to come down on me.

I separated myself. Like one of those poor lonely cougars that comes slinking out of the woods after spending its whole life leaping over fallen trees and living in caves, I crept out of the mountains little by little, going here and there, before finally coming to New York. Sometimes I feel as out of place and startled here as the coal-black mountain lions that occasionally found their way into my grandma's back yard. Enraged and frightened, she leveled her rifle at them, firing across the yard, aiming for their hearts.

Those cougars ran, heavy paws marking the dew-wet

grass, past the trees and garden and barn, back toward the impenetrable edge of the woods. Later, on those nights, when I could hear the slight, even snoring of my grandmother in the next room, I would fuck myself furiously, the silver moonlight falling across my face, my veins and heart tremulous, the yowling of those "painners" (my grandmaw's patois for *panther*) tearing at my ears.

There's a difference between growing up in the South and growing up in the mountains. Mountain people are rougher, darker, inundated by the shadows cast by ridges in dying light, marked by the fear of semis barreling down curving roads, their horns blaring a warning, scarred by coal mining and growing tobacco, or by growing nothing. The souls of mountain people are both larger and smaller, claustrophobic from dense woods and swollen with the views of wide valleys.

I never noticed this until I had an Appalachian lover. I knew there was something familiar about her face as soon as I met her, something that reeked of high school dances and homecoming, something that seemed so familiar that it was almost completely buried in memory. I knew her for months before I thought to ask her where she was from.

"West Virginia," she said.

The noise in the bar turned down for a moment. I looked at her again like I never had before.

"You're from Kentucky, right?"

"Yeah."

"Well, how the fuck about that," she said and raised her glass.

She was full of stories she told in a voice like thick smoke pouring from limbs too green to burn.

"I used to go out with this guy back in West Virginia," she said, leaning up against me, the cool pint glass she was holding beading moisture on my arm. "He wasn't too smart, but he was good looking. He had a nice car. He and I drove around a lot, looking for a place to fuck. I remember one night after school had just let out for the summer. His parents were home and my parents were home and all the spots we usually went were too crowded or too far away. I just wanted him to fuck me."

I closed my eyes and held onto my beer tighter. I imagined her pussy dense and wet and her lifting her skirt up a little, so that the cool night air blew against it.

"I got near crazy thinking about his cock hard in his blue jeans."

We were both drunk. I was able to close my eyes and get a clear picture of Maria as a teenager, fucking herself the way I had done years before. I laughed. "Did you hear panthers yelling when you did it?"

She looked at me and smiled. "I heard trains. Or I heard nothing. I heard darkness.

"So me and that boy drove around for a long time until he finally pulled up into the school parking lot. It was late and there wasn't a soul around. I tore at him. I wanted to get down to his bones. But it wasn't about him. It was about me.

"We opened up the doors and fell out onto the pavement. It started to hurt after a while, my back and thighs all cut up with gravel, his knees bruised. So he pulled me up on the trunk of his car and fucked me like that, my skirt up around my waist, his belt buckle making noise against the metal of the car."

She stopped and took a long drink of her beer and wiped off the little foam mustache. "He fucked me, and the whole time I thought about mountains and coal mining and boredom and football games and graduation....And then I thought about coming here."

"Why'd you want to come here?" I asked.

She waited a minute before she answered me. "Because I wanted that pent-up feeling to go away. I didn't want to be bored anymore. And I figured there'd be better places to fuck than high school parking lots."

That night on Avenue A she pressed my broad shoulders up against the rough bricks of a bodega. She pushed me and clung to me at the same time, her breath reeking of the good smell of whiskey and smoke. I felt the fury in her as she pressed me against the wall, daring me to shrug off her grip. Her hunger was almost frightening but I recognized it immediately. The mountains of New York are not as tall or dark as the ones in Appalachia. They seem easy to conquer after living through deprivation, silence, and fear.

She dug her coal-blackened fingers into my arms; they left smudges like maple leaves down my biceps. Her iron resolve reached beneath the wide black band of my belt. There was struggle in the way she held me, as if she'd been searching for something for so long she'd finally given up on it, then slowly begun to realize she'd found it.

Later that night as she lay deep asleep on my arm, I thought about the feeling she had described while telling her story, a suffocating thing like trying to breathe in a hot room, as irreproachable as thick clouds moving swiftly across the sky. I remembered the feeling well, something that had crept under my sheets at night in the summer, that had led me to walk doggedly through the silver-streaked woods in winter. Desire and boredom are transformed in the city; they appear in different ways. They can be stealthy, almost unrecognizable, until you find your heart is missing one and pressed flat by the other.

Fucking became consumptive after that. When I've spent some time with a lover, it becomes art. It's true that sex disappears almost immediately, does not even hang in the trees before disappearing into space, that it travels up through the air as unnoticed as the hot and sour breath of my grandma's ragged praying and my grandfather's strange and lonely Bible incantations. But while it's happening the air between us is transformed into an endless stream of words. Novels fly out of me in the course of an hour. The only one who will ever read them is the person I've delivered them to, my hand deep in her cunt, fingers in her mouth, her ass, brushing against her heart. I would like to see the words the air is tattooed with after it is over, as holy and sacred as the crisscrossed dim air in the cathedrals on Fifth Avenue. With everything, I want the intersection of what's really hard and what's unbearable, want the things that I do to her body to remind her that living is both futile and sweet.

"Everything means too much," she growled, spit soaking into the handkerchief I forced into her mouth. I slammed her body up against the wall, a metal dog leash linked to her collar wrapped around one fist. I am not sure when these things began to turn me on, when the darkness, violence, and beauty I hold within myself became embodied in certain strips of leather, a sharp point. I imagine drawing maps on her in blood. I don't do this, just threaten it, a sharp blade pressed up against her throat.

Bruises bloomed on my face weekly. They seemed to run blue and purple down my cheeks, to puff up in dark sunsets under my eyes. My arms were covered with teeth marks, mouth prints, and thumb and fist marks. They burned under the July sun. They faded into a strange tan. The way she touched my body opened up a new pathway to old memories that living in the city had covered up with deadlines, stress, and subway interiors.

The thing that resonated between us was the intersection of myth in our own lives. Between us was the unspoken memory of the mountains. Together we have a wildness in us that living in the city cannot touch. It's bigger than the color green. It's the muck that old leaves and twigs make when they clog up a stream, when they start to turn to earth in the water.

It's a tennis shoe, a rough worn Adidas getting caught in the mulch, the cold of the mud closing around our feet, destroying socks, painting ankles, hands clutching the resilient secretive bulbs of Easter flowers. It's thinking there are secrets and dangers hidden in the mountains, and dangers and secrets in the rest of the world. It's thinking there's something ancient that can't even be touched, ancient because down there we didn't know history beyond our own front door, didn't know religion besides getting hoisted up onto the back of a car and getting fucked.

My roommates, curious, asked me about my marks.

"What does she do to you?"

"Do you like that?"

"What do you do to *her*?"

We were sitting on the roof of our apartment, drinking beers, watching the neighborhood boys on the street below. I thought hard for a minute and pictures of us fucking came to me in flashes: her pointed red heels slamming into my chest, her fists pressing against my cheekbones, the brittle red lines she drew on my chest with razor blades. It was so much more precise and complicated than the sex I had envisioned myself having in high school, but it allowed me to revisit two parts of myself simultaneously: the wild, hungry part that had grown up in Kentucky, full of hope and loathing, and the part that had become exacting, hard, and small from living in New York.

I shrugged. I was scared to say the words out loud to them. Fucking her is like watching a thunderstorm roll in. The air is tremulous; it sings against my skin. The dark, heavy feeling just before the rain starts crawls all over me. I think of her shoved up on the back of that car in her high school parking lot. I see my high school then, the pavement slowly darkened by rain, the smell of dying leaves and green grass, and for a moment I want to go back. I see the acid stains left from leaves pressed wet against the sidewalk, feel the elation and exhaustion from seeking beauty in every little thing. With her ass in my face I almost touch the stories from my old life, and with my fist in her there is no denying history.

But it ain't all so serious, I want to tell them. There was a time when we were just two girls together, two girls who came dirty from the mountains, one of us beautiful and the other something else entirely, two girls who in the beginning just wanted a way to laugh, to be less lonely. The wanting came later, in bathrooms and pickup trucks and house parties. The wanting came later and would never quite go away.

Back in West Virginia Maria showed me the queer bars she used to go to downtown where the old queens hung out. The queer bar she went to before she'd ever thought about being queer, the letters written out in candy cane neon. She showed me the top of the hill where she'd drunk beer with the big-dicked guys she used to fuck in high school, and I showed her the walls of my father's house and the mountains around them, so far away from the coal stink of Charleston, West Virginia, and the noise of cars going over bridges.

Some people fuck to be free and some people fuck because they're penned in. Some people will claw your eyes out trying to get to themselves. Some people put their heart under the wheels of a car early on so they don't have to deal with it screaming at them later on. And some people will turn you inside out just to get you to really look at your pink insides.

There's all kinds of gospel to sing, and we did find something to sing, something that came out of both of us being born. We went back to the mountains that have our hearts and held each other by the throats on a dance floor in eastern Kentucky, swearing, *No matter what, I will not get old. No matter what, I will always love you.*

But those old queens, they could've told us, girl, your face will fade and those tits will sag and your love'll just move on to someone else until it ain't even love anymore. The candy neon lights will keep blinking, but you'll forget all of it, even the old high hills you used to go to, the loneliness so deep you could never cut out the root of it, the wind ice-knife sharp on the bridges over Charleston. Before those bridges, there were only mountains. And before anything else happened, we were just two girls looking for a good time. We didn't even know we were in love, just the way the mountains never know how they're loved, even if their beauty cripples the people around them.

Before the old queens' prophecy comes in and time does its dirty trick, we're animals rolling around in the wet green grass of my grandma's back yard, and Maria's dyed red hair is astonishing against our white skin. She's making grunting noises into my pussy, pressing her whole face into it, tongue stretched out. I become something else then and so does she, not getting beyond language, but before it.

I'd almost forgotten what it was like. A memory like something I'd forgotten from childhood, brought back by a certain smell, a color, a shift in the light of the room. The mountain lion came down out of the mountains, stirring up memory, sniffing the wild rivers hidden in the quiet currents of my blood. I grew claws. I sank them into the old bedspread on Maria's bed, felt the carpet furrow into the hard caps of my knees. Her breath was hot summer wind in my ear. It carried words and nonwords, it carried hate and love, affection and betrayal. Most of all it carried something pent-up, something about her that had spent years pacing the floor, wondering about the moon, something with dirt under its fingernails, from struggling, from clawing its way out. Her home lay in a valley like a grave in West Virginia. My own home in the mountains lay tiny in the back of my mind, almost obscured by the rush of my running away from it.

Maria hits me and it echoes through my stomach, pushes everything out of my lungs and throat. She pushes me forward, punching me again and again, little drops of sweat flying off her forehead. I feel like I'm being fucked everywhere at once. My cunt hisses and throbs. I sink my teeth into the bedspread. The sun is bright and dust-mottled. I think of a time I was left alone as a child in a Kmart parking lot. It was summertime and my mother had forgotten to roll down the windows. The cracked vinyl of her Oldsmobile stank. It was hot to the touch. I closed my eyes and imagined myself trapped, left to sweat away in the hot sun, the muscles of my cunt and ass tightening and relaxing. It was the first time I ever had an orgasm.

We are like two big cats wrestling, growling, screaming, our nails deep in each other's backs. It's only in these moments that I feel I am capable of any real violence. There is a terrible dark surge in me that I am somehow able to transform into pleasure. But there are slim moments when I tighten my belt too much, when I hit too hard, when I draw the knife too tight just because I can, just to see what will happen. It's a dangerous thing, a necessary thing, like pushing further past the edge of a wood that screams *impenetrable*. I know she understands why we do this; memory and history are what lie on the other side of that darkness.

The Tow
L. Shane Conner

Since my recent graduation I've been working for a uniform supply company in Columbus, Ohio. It's low stress and includes health insurance but it's kind of boring most of the time. I go in at five in the morning, pick up my truck, and drive around the countryside delivering uniforms to various businesses. I'm supposed to try to sell more than they actually order but usually they're not interested. The scenery is mostly cows and cornfields, and a lot of the businesses are run by good old boys and garden variety rednecks. But I get weekends off and I don't have to wear femme drag, which is good since I'm a wimp when it comes to heels.

One morning a couple of weeks ago a deer ran in front of my truck. I hit the brakes, swerved, and ended up in a field of corn that looked like a battlefield graveyard with the mud and broken, brown stalks. For a long, quiet minute I sat still behind the wheel, staring at the dashboard, my heart pounding, and the adrenaline making me shake. At fifty miles an hour, when the truck came up on two wheels, I'd been sure it was going to roll. When I got out to survey the damage, everything looked pretty much okay except that I was thirty or forty feet off the road ankle deep in mud and there was no way I was going to be able to drive back out.

The tow truck took at least half an hour to get there and when it did, it turned out one of my axles was broken and the truck wasn't drivable. My company said one of the other drivers could pick me up around four and he'd call when he was on the way. I looked at my watch: eleven-thirty. The nearest town was only the size of a couple of city blocks, and I had at least four hours to kill. I leaned my head back against the seat of the tow truck and closed my eyes. The tow truck guy got in then and asked me if I was all right.

"Yeah, I'm just stuck out here until at least four and I feel like an idiot for running off the road just to avoid a deer."

"Don't worry about it," he said. "Happens all the time. They do just as much damage if you hit 'em." There was a long silence while he put his truck in gear and pulled off the narrow shoulder onto the road. "You're welcome to join me for lunch. I mean, there's a diner in town with pretty good food and I'm going over there anyway as soon as I drop the truck off at the garage."

I guess because I'd been shaken by the accident I hadn't paid much attention to the tow truck guy. He had on baggy work clothes with a ball cap pulled low over his eyes. His name tag said he was CHRIS, and even though his voice was deep with a rough edge to it he barely even had what could pass for peach fuzz on his cheeks. He looked like he still belonged in high school. He seemed like a nice, polite kid and the diner looked like something out of a movie with a happy ending so I followed him down the block from his garage and across the street. When he held the door for me I almost thought he was flirting. He wasn't that much younger, but then I thought I was probably flattering myself. I'm a little too jock and a little too butch to appeal to most young guys.

I realized my mistake as soon as he took his hat off. My tow truck boy was a woman. I never would have missed it in the city. I guess queer people live everywhere, but I never really picture us as part of small-town life. Sure, maybe she wasn't queer. Maybe she was passing as a boy, maybe she was in transition. She looked butcher than I think I do, and people mistake me for a guy all the time, even gay men once in a while.

We drank coffee while we waited for our food. I remember she took hers black but I can't remember anything we talked about during lunch. The more I looked at her, the more I couldn't believe I'd mistaken her for a boy. Her hands were strong but they weren't a man's hands, and there was something very pretty about her eyes. She caught me staring at her but she just smiled and kept right on eating. We finally started really talking while we walked back to the garage, though as shallow as it sounds, I think I asked her questions mainly just to hear her voice.

It turned out her father had owned the garage and she'd grown up working on cars with him. When she was eighteen she'd gone away to college but when he died of cancer a few years later, she'd come back to run the garage and take care of her mother, who started getting senile the day her father died. I still didn't know how to broach the subject of being queer. I kept getting distracted by little things about her and I felt self-conscious, which is not the way I usually feel around women. It's not that I'm the hottest girl around, it's just that I've always been sure I could please a woman—any woman. It sounds vain when I say it, but it's not a matter of having some great technique so much as really, sincerely wanting to please women.

I felt like an awkward kid with her and I couldn't figure out why. I tried not to fidget and play with my clothes while she unlocked the side door of the garage and stepped back to let me in. Then it hit me. I'm always the one who holds the door, the one who carries the heavy boxes. I'm not stone, but when I meet a woman I'm attracted to I want to have her, to taste her, to feel her body move beneath my hands, to hear her voice change when she comes. I wanted this woman to take *me*, and it was a new and powerful feeling.

Inside the garage it was warm and she took off her work shirt, stripping down to an old stained tank top. She was thin, but the muscles in her shoulders and arms stood out in strong, clean lines. I tried to be nonchalant, eyeballing a really old car I couldn't believe still ran while she did something or other in the garage's small office. When she came back out she told me she planned to restore the car to its original 1958 glory. She already had it running, now all it needed was fine-tuning and a lot of body work. She came toward me while I was running my hand over the rough, unfinished primer that covered the hood.

I thought she was trying to squeeze past but she stopped, almost touching me, the heat of our bodies mingling between us, palpable as a third skin. My breath caught in my throat, which is something I thought only happened to beautiful female leads in old movies with long dancing scenes. Her eyes caught mine. I wanted her, and I was sure she knew it. Before I could say anything she brought her hand up between my legs, hard. My ass hit the cool cinder block of the wall behind me, followed by one of her fingers finding my clit through my pants. She lifted my chin with her other hand and kissed my neck. Her fingers traced the line of my jaw, her thumb ran along my lower lip.

She stopped abruptly, leaned back, and looked down at my feet. "Why don't you kick your shoes off," she said in a voice that was more a command than a request.

I hesitated maybe a second. As soon as my shoes were off

she had my pants and underwear down around my ankles. She turned me and put me up on the hood of the car, lifting me with surprising ease. It was cold against the bare skin of my ass, colder than the wall had been and smoother. I could still feel her hand pressing into me.

She ran a finger between the folds of my labia and smiled as she felt the wetness there. I could see her pulse on the side of her throat, but I couldn't look any higher than the corners of her mouth, still couldn't get myself to meet her eyes. She pulled me forward by the front of my shirt and kissed me full on the lips, her tongue in my mouth almost immediately, not forceful but curious, exploring. When she pulled away again she had unbuttoned my shirt and now she slid it off over my shoulders, followed it with the boy's large tank top I wear in place of a bra.

She pushed me down into the steel hood, fondling my breasts, kneading with her calloused palms. Without hurting, her touch communicated strength. My feet were still resting on the broad fender as my back pressed against the hood. Smooth cold metal traced a new crease into the muscle of my thigh. As the weight of the thing fell across my belly I could see that it was some kind of wrench, rounded at both ends and nearly a foot and a half long. My body jumped and the muscles of my inner thighs contracted involuntarily as she ran the handle between my legs, pushing the hood back from my swelling clit. She eased the long handle inside me and I thought about objecting. I meant to. Then she tilted the end up and found my G-spot. She wasn't fucking me with the wrench so much as massaging the spot while her left hand continued to explore every inch of my skin within reach. The pads of her fingers drew the tense edges of my nipples taut and I felt myself finally begin to press back against her.

When I came she slid the wrench away, setting it gently on the floor. Then I felt her mouth on me. She brought my knees up over her shoulders as she buried her face between my legs. Her tongue probed my cunt, working its way up, circling my clit, pressing the glans into the back of her front teeth. Then she slipped her tongue inside the clit hood and drew the swelling flesh out from the folds surrounding it. She flicked her tongue over my clit in a growing rhythm, then sucked it deep into her mouth. After I came a second time, my hands over my head, holding onto the top edge of the hood of the car, squeezing her head between my thighs, she picked me up and carried me to the other side of the garage. She didn't even seem to struggle as she walked up the stairs, holding me in her arms like a child.

I don't know what I thought the upstairs room would look like, but I was surprised. I guess maybe I expected something like a college student décor, or a stereotypical bachelor pad. The only posters were framed prints, Van Gogh and Georgia O'Keefe. There were no beer cans or old liquor bottles in sight, and the book shelf was more dominant than the television. It was a large room, with a Japanese style folding screen at one end in front of the bed. She set me gently on the bed and for a while we just kissed as she let me begin to explore her body. I liked the shape of her muscles and I liked the shape of her breasts too. I sucked on her nipples, I kissed every piece of skin I could reach with my mouth, and gradually I eased her stained, navy work pants open. They slid easily over her narrow hips but I had to kneel on the floor to untie her boots before I could pull everything free.

I eased her boxers off separately, pausing to look at her when I did. The beautiful woman's shape that had been hidden under her clothes left me feeling reverent, as though I were viewing some special, secret place. I kissed the hollow at the inside edge of her hip bone first, slowly moving down to the crease where her leg ended in the dark brown curls of her pubic hair. I could smell the light scent of her and, though I had expected to have to work hard to turn her on, I found her already wet. She ran her fingers through my hair as I ran the tip of my tongue down between her outer labia. I pulled them slowly apart as I probed deeper, exploring, learning the shape of her. I began to experiment with my technique, wondering if she was really enjoying it. Suddenly her hand gripped the back of my head, barely catching in my short hair, and I knew I'd found the right spot—but she was still quiet. Even when she came, only small gasps escaped. I knew I could get her to be louder if she gave me the chance.

We held each other for a long time. At first we didn't talk, only traced each other's bodies with gentle fingers as we kissed slow and long. When we did begin talking it seemed like we were able to be easy and familiar without trying. We'd read a lot of the same books and had a lot of the same favorites. We decided to see each other again on the weekend. She said she could drive up to Columbus on Friday night and stay through Sunday. Fortunately there came a lull in our conversation when my cell phone rang or I wouldn't have heard it. It was still clipped onto my pants downstairs on the garage floor. Donnie was coming to pick me up and he thought he'd be there in about twenty minutes. After I'd put my clothes back on I called him back and gave him the address. We kissed and cuddled inside the garage until we heard Donnie honk out front, then we hugged one last time and I left, promising to call her the next day.

An Australian Rodeo

Eva Hore

Hearing sirens wailing I looked up into the rear-view mirror to see a cop car, right up the arse of my car. Its headlights and emergency lights flashed crazily. Looking down I saw I was doing 135 kilometers per hour.

"Oh, shit. Fuck it!" I said.

Sonja, who had been sleeping, sat up, immediately alarmed.

"What happened? What's going..."

"It's the cops again," I said, pulling over to the emergency lane. "Where'd he come from?"

The car pulled in behind me, blue lights still flashing but the siren turned off.

We were on our way to Wodonga, near the border of New South Wales. A rodeo was on this weekend, and we'd decided to pool our money to have one last adventure before going home to England. It wasn't quite in the outback, but nevertheless it was still high country to us.

I checked the side mirror. What do you know, a female. Butch-looking, too. She walked confidently toward the driver's door.

I hitched up my skirt and quickly opened the buttons of my shirt, exposing most of my breasts.

"Hi, officer," I said.

"Do you realize you were doing 135 kilometers in a 110 kilometer zone?" she asked.

"No, I didn't," I said wide-eyed. "Are you sure?"

"You can come and look at the speedometer reading if you wish."

"Okay," I said, opening my legs wide and giving her an eyeful as I alighted from the car.

She pointed through the window to her dash. I leaned right over, knowing my skirt would ride high enough to expose my cheeks. I was wearing a G-string.

"Oh, shit," I said. "I can't believe it."

"Hmm," she said.

I knew she must have been checking out my arse.

"I can't believe it. I just got a two-hundred-dollar fine on the spot, about a hundred kilometers back."

"Not your lucky day, is it?" she said.

"No," I said sweetly, coming in closer.

"You girls from England?" she asked flipping the pad open.

"Yeah."

"How much longer you down here?" she asked, scribbling down details from my license.

"This is our last weekend in Victoria. We're flying out to Brisbane on Monday afternoon, to hook up with our international flight back home. We pooled all our money together for the rodeo and now we'll have none left for accommodation."

"That's bad luck."

"We were hoping to get someone to put us up for the weekend—you know, in exchange for some housework?"

She paused in her writing and looked at me. She seemed to be considering something and I was hoping she was going to let us go.

"Look," she said. "I have to fine you. I logged into the computer I was giving chase."

"Oh," I said, looking miserable.

"I'm actually on duty at the rodeo tomorrow. But I've got a big place. I can put you both up over the weekend and you can help me around the house."

"Really?" I asked, excited.

"Yeah. Look I'll make the fine the minimum, which is fifty dollars. I was on my way home for lunch anyway, so you can follow me there."

"Gee, thanks, I really appreciate it. By the way, my name's Melissa," I said holding out my hand.

"I know," she said, with a slight smirk. "I read it on the license. I'm Tanya. Come on, let's get going."

Hopping back into the car, I told Sonja what had happened.

"You idiot," she said. "I told you to slow down. You should have let *me* drive." She was angry about having to pay another fine.

"Yeah, well, we can't do anything about it now, can we? At least we have somewhere to stay, and maybe she can get us into the rodeo for free."

"Well, I'm not doing much housework. I wasn't the one speeding, remember." She had overheard our deal.

"Yeah, yeah," I said, following Tanya slowly. I noticed she was doing precisely the speed limit.

She had a huge farm, its pastures full of sheep, cattle, and horses. She was breeding Arabians and was delighted to show us around.

She still had five hours of duty to perform, and after giving us a tour of the farmhouse and a quick lunch, she left.

The house was a mess, but I was determined to do a good job. Being friendly with a police officer was always a good idea, and if she could get us in to the rodeo...well, that would be a bonus.

I carefully snooped around her bedroom, going through cupboards and drawers. There weren't any photos around of old boyfriends, and in one of the drawers I found dildos, toys, and a snappy little whip.

Looks like my hunch about her was right. Maybe this weekend would turn out better than I'd anticipated.

Sonja was straight, unfortunately. We'd been friends since preschool. Made me sick to think she'd let guys up into that fabulous pussy, but hey, each to their own.

In our teenage years we'd fooled around together a bit, like most girls do. I found her body irresistible but she wasn't interested in me that way. I'd begged her to let me show her what my tongue could do, now that I was more experienced, but she just wasn't interested.

Now I heard the distant sound of thunder rolling around the valley, and the smell of rain was in the air. I took the liberty of cooking dinner for the three of us. I waited for Tanya to return. Sonja went to bed early.

Tayna arrived home just as a north wind picked up, scaring the horses. We ran out to the stables and herded them into their stalls. They were snorting and pawing at the sawdust and hay, which lay strewn amongst their stalls.

I watched fascinated as she tried to calm them down. They were such huge beasts. They had a skittishness about them as though they knew something more than that a storm was going to happen.

We fed them fresh grain and oats, which settled them down. We put the food back into the tack room and I looked around at the variety of bridles, whips, and lassoes. It was a great room, full of history and stories, I'd venture to bet.

The earsplitting boom of thunder shook the stables. The stallions neighed, pawing at the ground. I looked at her and noticed a girlishness I hadn't seen before. We stared at each other. The whole atmosphere was charged as the sky opened up and heavy splats of rain hit the old tin roof.

I moved toward her. She stood still, breathing heavily. I ran my finger down her cheek and onto her lips. Her mouth opened and sucked my finger deep inside, her tongue rolling around it.

Good, she was keen and submissive, just how I liked my girls.

I grabbed her by the nape of the neck, wrenching her backward. My mouth sought out the hollow in her throat and I licked gently at it, then traveled slowly downward into the cleavage of her bra where I nipped at the swell of her breasts.

She moaned.

With my other hand I grabbed the front of her shirt, ripping the buttons off, startling her. Her breath was coming out quickly now as I peeled the shirt off her shoulders and down her arms and discarded it onto the floor.

A block and tackle was hanging from the ceiling, a rope dangling from it. I raised her arms above her head and tied her tightly to it. She was balancing on the tip of her toes as she swayed back and forth.

I undid her belt, noting the empty holster where her gun would normally rest. I removed the officer's baton from its clasp and placed it on a bale of hay. Slowly I pulled down her zip and yanked her trousers down. She kicked at her feet, slipping off her shoes, and I pulled the trousers off her.

All she was left in was her bra, panties, and socks. There was a look of wild passion in her eyes now as she licked her dry lips.

"Hmm," I murmured.

I left her there and inspected the tack room, looking for what I needed. I found an old pair of shears, rusty and brown. I pulled a saddle over and, under a blanket, discovered a small but sturdy whip.

As the thunder rolled about outside, the horses resumed

their neighing. I looked over at the stallion as it rose up on its hind legs, pawing the air. It was a magnificent beast. Lightning flashed, rain continued to pelt down, deafening us for a moment with their ferocity.

Moving back toward her I undid my shirt, dropping it onto the floor with her clothes. I removed my skirt, enjoying her intake of her breath when she saw my black G-string and matching bra.

Standing before her, I unclipped the back of my bra and let it fall to the ground. My breasts swayed, happy for the release. I lifted them toward her, massaging them as her mouth and tongue sought me out, eager to taste my flesh.

I laughed and pulled back, teasing her, then crushed my breasts into her face. Her hot wet mouth sucked at my nipples, her tongue flicked around crazily, her legs were trying to wrap around me, pull me into her. I moved away from her hungry mouth and carefully chose an item from atop the hay bale.

I took the rusty shears and pushed them up and under the front of her bra. It wouldn't cut straight through, just tugged at the material, so I pulled hard and felt it rip. This allowed her small breasts to escape the tightness of the straps as they'd been pulled upward, straining from the rope.

Her bra hung haphazardly under her armpits while I took the shears again and slid them down the front of her panties. She sucked in, pulling in the podgy little stomach as though fearing I would cut her skin.

Again, I worked the handles of the shears to no avail, making only a slight nick in the fabric. Throwing them to the floor I pulled hard at the front of her panties, ripping them apart, leaving them to fall to her ankles for her to discard.

She was totally naked now. Swaying with desire. Her breasts were small; nipples dark and firm, her hips wide, legs stocky, and she had a wide bush of pubic hair. No waxing for this girl.

I ran my fingers through her bush, spreading out the hair, enjoying the coarseness of it, so unlike my own hair-free pussy. She opened her legs, inviting me in, but I had other plans.

I took the black baton and ran it from her ankle up the inside of her leg, straying over her pussy, and then down the other leg. She arched herself toward me, her legs opening as wide as she could, in her position.

I took the baton and slipped it down my own panties, rubbing it up and down my clit.

"Oh, that feels good," I said, eyeing her for a reaction.

The bulge of the baton in my tight G-string, rubbing up and down, heightened my own desire. I slipped it further down, allowing it to part my lips and touch the opening of my pussy. I was wet, so very wet.

Coming closer I pushed myself into her, as the baton, cloaked in the silk of my G-string, rubbed against her pussy.

"Let me down, please," she begged. "I'll do anything."

"Not yet," I said.

I took the baton and placed it at her lips. Her mouth opened as she sucked it, licking off my juices.

I peeled my G-string down and brought it over the saddle. I sat on it, riding it with my naked pussy, enjoying the sensation. Then I leaned back, opening my legs and giving her an eyeful as I slowly pushed the tip of the baton inside me.

She was rubbing her legs together, trying to get some friction on her hot pussy. I watched her watch me as I slipped it in deeper. My lips swelled as the blood pulsated around it. Further and further I pushed, opening my legs wider, using only one hand so I could rub my clit at the same time.

The rain continued to pelt the old roof, but the thunder was settling, allowing the horses to calm down a bit. The stallion, though, pawed at the hay-strewn ground, watching us with wild eyes. The smell of manure, hay, and rain wafted around me, bringing out a raw earthiness to match our desire.

I felt an orgasm building, my juices wetting the saddle. Removing the baton, again I rode the saddle, slipping over it much more easily now, my clit electrified, my knees pressed into the ground.

I rose slowly, taking the baton and slipping it between her thick thighs. I rubbed it into and out of her pussy lips, not allowing it to enter her completely. She was so hot she climaxed almost at once.

She hung there panting, her head falling backward, her arms stretched out as her legs hung limply. I kissed her neck, my tongue tracing its way to her mouth. As our lips locked, our tongues sought out the other's. We kissed with a passion I hadn't felt for many months.

Again I went to the hay bale, but this time I brought back the whip. Her eyes widened, as I flicked her gently on the hip. Harder now, I flicked her arms, breasts, and stomach, and as she moved sideways I gave her arse a hard flick, noting how quickly the welts rose on her fevered skin.

Over her breasts, under her arms, and as she opened her legs I flicked carefully, not wanting to hurt, only to excite her passion even more.

I snaked the handle of the whip up her legs and pushed it quickly into her hot wet pussy.

"Oh, God, yes," she moaned. "Yes."

In and out, deeper and deeper, until she cried out. I watched as her juices slid down, wetting the threads of leather as she came again.

Then I attacked her breasts, biting into her nipples, sucking and licking them. I held onto her arse, kneading the cheeks, opening them, running my fingers down her crack, pulling her into my body.

"For God's sake, let me down," she pleaded. "I want to hold and touch you. I need to feast on your pussy. Please untie me."

I laughed. I too wanted her mouth on me, but not quite yet. There was a ladder in the corner of the room, so I sauntered over there, dragging it back with me and placing it before her.

I climbed up, slowly letting my arse caress her body as I climbed. Before I got to the top, her tongue sought out my hole and I felt her hot mouth biting, sucking, and licking me feverishly, as though she was starved.

Turning around I leaned my body into her face, my naked pussy directly over her mouth. Opening my legs slightly I saw her tongue stretch out toward me. I waited as she struggled to get closer to me. She could only manage to reach the tip of my pussy, my clit. Then I planted my arse on the ladder and smothered her face into me.

God, it was heaven, balancing up there with her hungry mouth eating me, lapping, nibbling, and sucking. Pushing in a bit closer I felt another orgasm gush into her open mouth. She sucked, licked, and swallowed, tantalizing my clit with her wonderful mouth.

When I'd finally had enough I untied her hands and her arms fell limply at her side. She recovered quickly and practically threw me onto the ground, attacking every part of me with gusto.

Her hands were kneading my breasts, then quickly exploring my pussy, only to be replaced by her mouth. She was so hot. I rolled her off me and lay on top of her, our pussies covering each other's mouths.

With fingers and tongues exploring each other we came again and again, eventually collapsing together on the hay-covered floor.

Later, she invited me into her bedroom. I already knew she had a huge spa there and was delighted when she filled it, suds cascading onto the floor as we wrestled in the water.

"Oh, Tanya," I said, as she lifted me onto the edge of the spa. "Are all you small-town cops this horny?"

"Only when something as hot as you comes speeding into town," she said with a laugh.

Her tongue was exploring me as fingers gently opened my swollen lips. Darting in and out, I leaned back, legs spread, and let her do what she did best.

She rolled me over, water running down my arse as her tongue licked around my hole. Her fingers massaged my asscheeks, then slipped toward my clit where she rubbed furiously. I fell back into the water as the most wonderful orgasm gushed out of me.

We held each other for a few moments, my legs open, straddling her waist. Then she whispered to me.

"What would Sonja think if she came in here?"

"Sonja's straight, unfortunately," I said. "I've been trying to convert her for years."

"I'd love to see her naked. Do you think she'd join us?" she asked.

"We could try. She has the most gorgeous pussy. If you can find her a horny cop, maybe she'd join us for a foursome."

"I know just the guy," she said.

"You know that rodeo tomorrow?" I said. "Why don't you call in sick and we can do some riding of our own."

And we sure did. But hey, that's another story.

Sunset, Sunrise
Sacchi Green

Oh, damn, I had it bad this time! And no way in hell would the truck that had hit me pull over to take me for a ride.

I'll never be old enough to know better. "I'll take table six," I hissed at Audrey as she passed my office door. "Don't worry, you'll get the tip. And it'll be a good one."

So much for avoiding temptation this summer. No Provincetown beaches for me, or clubs and babydykes on training wheels. With my life at long last cleared of distractions, I needed to focus on my Wellfleet studio and the restaurant bookkeeping job that pays the bills. But if trouble had come looking for me, how could I look away?

Not that Trouble, with a definite capital *T*, was actually looking my way. The big salt-and-pepper butch had eyes (and hands—such broad, strong hands!) only for the gorgeous young redhead who made *voluptuous* seem like a four-letter word.

Audrey sized up the situation fast. "So what else do I get?"

"All right," I muttered, "come around, tomorrow night." Audrey might be more intriguing if her interests weren't strictly confined to getting her posterior paddled. I always make her earn it.

At table six I stood at the young lady's shoulder, gazing deliberately down into the lush cleavage revealed by clinging azure silk. Then I glanced at her companion, hoping for a reaction. It didn't even much matter what kind.

Clear hazel eyes in a sun-ruddy face surveyed me with a hint of amusement, and recognition.

"Good evening, I'm Rory," I said demurely. "I'll be serving you tonight."

The corners of her mouth twitched. (Her? Sir, on occasion, without doubt; definitely a Daddy; but yes, in my own private lexicon, Her.)

"Hi, Rory," she said. "You must be moonlighting. Didn't we last see you covered in mud?"

"Close enough," I acknowledged. "Art feeds the soul, but that's about all."

I'd been smeared with clay when they'd wandered through the collective gallery that afternoon and glanced into my studio, obviously looking for a corner just secluded enough that they could pretend no one might see them making out. The butch had resisted the kid's tug on her muscle-T long enough to look appreciatively at my nudes in porcelain and stone. "Go ahead," I'd said, as her hand hovered over the rounded marble ass of a full-bodied figure crouching on all fours. "Go on, it's meant to be irresistible."

The carnal magnetism of her grin had hit me like pounding surf. When her big finger stroked the smooth buttocks and probed down between the tempting thighs, my crotch got wet enough to dampen the clay dust layering my jeans.

"Must have been quite some model," she had said appreciatively, ignoring the pout of jealousy quivering on her girl's full red lips.

"So's yours," I had said, looking boldly over the delectable young flesh my sculptures could only symbolize. This got me a sultry look through the girl's long lashes and a reassessment of my weathered androgyny, but Daddy had just laughed and steered her back into the hallway.

My imagination had seethed with visions of those large hands kneading and squeezing tender breasts and belly and thighs. The girl's shorts had been brief enough to reveal rosy traces of the proprietary bar-code Daddy's hand had imprinted on her naughty ass, with possible assistance from the back of a hairbrush. They must be staying somewhere close enough to have indulged in a bit of after-lunch action before taking a stroll through the galleries.

When they'd gone I stepped out into the hall for a moment just to immerse myself in the space that large, solid body had occupied. I could feel her primal energy flowing through me. My hands tingled with the remembrance of contours never actually touched.

Cadillac Mountain granite from Maine, speckled pink and gray, I thought, sketching furiously in my mind. But something deeper than thought flooded me with a longing to feel her generous flesh against mine. I would run my tongue from lips to jaw to throat and down between her breasts, licking sea salt and sweat from her skin, hearing in her low moans, as I probed and explored, the swelling of the tide I hungered desperately to taste....

Well. Another case of lust at first sight, with no expectation of repeat sightings. I'd scanned the crowds on the sidewalks and at the beach for the rest of the day, anyway, but saw no imposing figure with granite-gray hair, moving with just that confident set of head and shoulders and hips that had imprinted itself on me. Not until right now, tonight, in this four-star, white-linen-and-crystal-goblet restaurant.

I couldn't resist. "Would you like to order appetizers while you consider the entrées? The Chatham Oysters on the Half

Shell are especially plump and juicy tonight, and the Ceviche of Wellfleet Bay Scallops is, as always, superb."

"Excellent," Daddy said firmly, laying a casual hand over the girl's smaller one. "We'll have one of each, and share."

The girl looked suspiciously at the menu. "At least those snails last night were cooked," she muttered, then stifled a gasp as Daddy's hand on her wrist tightened. My hunch had been correct. Raw seafood was way outside the youngster's comfort zone.

"The lime juice in the ceviche has the same effect as cooking," I told her smoothly, and, to do her credit, she murmured faintly that it sounded very nice.

I couldn't dislike her, in spite of her youth, her sensuous beauty, and that she was just what Daddy wanted. The role-playing itself evoked only a lingering nostalgia; after all, I'd been on both sides of the equation, at one time or another. My hunger now was for an intensity driven by a common weight of years, of life, of howling pleasure into the teeth of mortality. All right, what I really needed was to get laid by someone who could give me what I wanted, and could handle what I wanted to give.

Not that there was any chance I'd get it. But I played my own game as I served them attentively. A dropped oyster fork was promptly replaced next to the girl's scarlet-tipped, manicured hand—with a private reflection that, judging by the length of the nails, I knew what Daddy wasn't getting, presumably by choice. An errant napkin was retrieved and allowed to drift briefly against the naked swell of breasts above the azure silk décolletage before it was restored to her lap.

Daddy saw me watching for her reaction. Did she know that with every glance at the girl I pictured an older, stronger body pressed against her, large hands pressing and tightening on full breasts, smooth shoulders, dampening thighs? Or was I staring too hungrily at her firm lips when she brushed her napkin across them? Her eyes held mine as her fingers deliberately relaxed and let the linen slide down over shirt and tie to her wide lap, and then to the floor.

I bent swiftly to pick it up, stroking her hip in passing, then stood behind her with my breasts nudging against her back as I leaned forward to spread the white cloth across her thighs. She turned to thank me, leaning her shoulder into me, and I saw in her upturned face that she felt the current of sensuality, knew perfectly well what I was up to, and was amused.

I started to move away for a fresh carafe of coffee. "Rory, just a minute," Daddy said. "Are there any evening activities around here you'd especially recommend to visitors?"

"Aren't we going to Provincetown, to the clubs?" the girl blurted out, and then subsided under a stern look.

I listed a few theatrical and musical events of a sedate and worthy nature, then told the truth as I saw it. "On a summer night like this, there's nothing more beautiful than watching the sunset from the beach on Chequesset Neck. If you're here tomorrow you should try it. It's already too late now." I nodded toward the view from the front window where the sky's afterglow still tinted the rivulets winding through the marsh with a russet sheen.

"All right, it's the bright lights of P'town tonight," she told the anxious girl. "Maybe we'll catch the sunset tomorrow and then make an early night of it before the long drive home."

Only here for the weekend, I thought. Figures. So much for my looking for trouble.

And then Trouble turned again in her seat and looked up at me. "Do you ever get time off to watch the sunset, Rory?" she asked.

"Once in a while. But even on my nights off I usually work in my studio. I'll be there late tonight, sketching out a project that's begun to obsess me." I looked from the hands resting on her broad thighs slowly up along her body to her face. If the sun hadn't already reddened her skin I'd have suspected that she was blushing.

"Maybe you could draw me a map to this sunset beach," she said. "Just in case." She turned to the girl. "Juliana, you run along to the ladies' room. I'll be with you in a minute."

I stepped close and pressed against her side. Her head was level with my breasts as I leaned over the table; my nipples tightened at the thought that her warm breath would brush them if she turned toward me.

Since linen napkins were out of bounds as scrap paper, I drew a map on a page from my order book. When I started to embellish it with a sketch of the sun setting over Boston across the bay, her large hand grasped mine and moved it, pen and all, to the lower edge of the paper.

"So your studio would be about...here?" she murmured.

I moved both our hands across the tablecloth a few inches. "Here," I said, nudging the salt shaker. "Where you saw me earlier." And then Juliana was beside us, the check was settled, and they were gone.

The night was warm even at two A.M. I stood outside my studio flexing stiff shoulders and fingers and watching the high, white moon sail above the salt marsh. Sketches sprawled across my drawing board, of hands, the set of a head, the turn of broad back and shoulders.

A car came down the deserted street, approached, slowed.... I didn't look around, didn't let myself hope, didn't move.

"Still obsessed by that project?" she asked, her breath warm against my ear.

"It's coming along." I moved to face her. "When I find just the right piece of granite, I'll know what to strip away to get at what I want."

"Wait a minute, you're not going to cut anything off, are you?" Shirt and tie had been left behind, along with the presumably sleeping girl whose musk still clung to Daddy.

I grasped the ribbed undershirt and tugged it upward.

"Not unless it won't go willingly," I said, and yanked it off over her cropped hair. My mouth pressed fiercely over hers to hold back whatever she might try to say. I got her belt unbuckled and my fingers inside her damp boxer shorts before she counterattacked, grabbing both my wrists in one big hand and stretching them up high while the other hand unbuttoned my shirt.

"Don't forget I'm an expert with a chisel," I panted, and ducked my head to set my teeth where neck met shoulder. She tasted of sweat and smoke and sea air. I scraped down across her chest to the swell of a breast, left a suction mark on its inner curve, and moved along to an insistent nipple. No more resistance, just her groans and sharper cries as I chewed her flesh to soreness, and my own gasps at the harsh clutch of her hands on my back and buttocks.

I lifted my head to blurt, "Inside!"

"How deep?" she shot back, gripping my crotch so hard I yipped like a pup.

"Whatever you can handle," I managed to get out. "But in there," jerking my head toward the interior of my studio.

We tumbled onto the futon in the corner. I'd left lube and gloves handy beside it, just in case.

She won the race to strip away what remained of each other's clothing, yanking my sweatpants off in one sweeping motion and swatting my ass hard before I rolled over and got my fingers hooked into her loosened belt. I slid to my knees on the floor and tugged, and she had to cooperate or be hobbled. As soon as her boxer shorts cleared her knees I had my head between her strong thighs, forcing them apart, pushing toward her pungent heat; she could have crushed me, but when I nipped at the tender skin near her crotch she leaned back with a gusty sigh and opened to me.

Her coppery bush was still untouched by gray. I licked my

way across her full lips and whipped at her straining clit with my tongue, hard and fast, until her hips arched high and her moans quickened.

I needed a deeper taste. My fingers took over externally, letting my tongue probe into her hot, slippery cunt until her groans and curses demanded more, and I reversed again, giving her two fingers, then three, easing in my whole fist. Her muscles clenched around it, and her full-throated, jubilant cry rang through her flesh into mine.

I'd barely retrieved my hand when she rolled onto me, shoving her thigh between my legs, working my nipples savagely while I bucked against her greater bulk. "Inside!" I demanded again. "Deep!" Her large finger moved skillfully into me. "More! All of it!" I begged. "I can handle it, dammit, give it to me!" Through my haze of need I saw her doubt, until I took in her whole hand, gradually at first, and with increasing urgency—and then I couldn't see anything at all, gripped by rolling waves of intensity.

I'd been wrong about the sunset. Dawn over her shoulder as we lay entangled was the most beautiful sight I'd ever seen. And the saddest.

Wordlessly I memorized her taste, my lips and tongue and teeth tracing the contours of her throat and collarbone. She drew in a deep breath, her chest rising beneath my mouth, but there was nothing to be said.

While she dressed, I slipped last night's sketches into a folder and handed it to her before she left. "For Juliana," I'd scrawled across it. "This is all for you."

I kept what was mine alone. There were more sketches, stored in my imagination, in my fingertips: views of her lover that she would never see, on the page or in the flesh.

As the car purred along the deserted street, I wrenched my mind away from what couldn't be, and toward the quest for just the right piece of solid granite.

Waterbaby
Elaine Miller

"'Complete nudity in itself is not erotic,'" Frankie read aloud from the hammock chair nearby. "'It becomes so only when preceded by or contrasted to a state of dress.'"

I spoke to the dishwater in which my arms were immersed, as I watched sweat trickle down my biceps, intent on joining the suds. "Complete nudity in itself is necessary to proper temperature regulation," I said in rejoinder. "All else is folly. Tell me why we rented this place in the hottest month of the year? I'm about to melt and drip down my own legs."

"Ooh, dripping thighs," she cried. I looked up and she presented me with a caricature of a sexy vamp look that dissolved into her usual giggle. Pulling her legs up and resting her elbows on her widespread knees, she smirked into her magazine. If I wasn't so damn hot and sweaty I'd consider the view heart-stopping.

"Look," she said. "This article goes on to say that since nudity is not erotic, clothes could be considered immoral. Does that make us upstanding moral beings?"

"No, girlie mine. You're an amoral wench no matter *what*

you're not wearing," I said, pulling the sink plug and wiping most of the water off my arms with a towel. I took a swipe or two at my belly and breasts, then gave up when I realized that those droplets were sweat, which would simply replace themselves if wiped away. A few steps out of the kitchenette brought me to the guesthouse's sitting room, and with a groan I dropped heavily onto the rattan couch, lay back, and closed my eyes.

"That piece of most outrageous flattery will get you kissed," I heard her say, then heard the rustle of the hammock chair and a moment later felt Frankie crawling up my belly, her sweet and familiar body soft and sweaty and...hot!

"God, girl, get off me!" I said, hurriedly picking her off my chest and tumbling her to the floor. "Let me cool off a bit." I hadn't opened my eyes but I felt her pout as clearly as if I was seeing her.

"Fine," she said. "I'll go take a shower and cool off, you big butch brute."

Her footsteps receded and I sighed. Her pouts never lasted more than a few minutes. I sprawled a little more comfortably, pulling my heavy breasts up with both hands so the undersides would air-dry, then drowsed off to the sound of the shower.

And came fully awake with a most unbutchly shriek. Cold! I blinked to clear cold water streaming down my face, and gaped at Frankie, who stood stark naked and grinning and holding a half-full bucket. I screamed again as she tossed the remaining water on me, the shock of cold intolerable on my overheated skin. Then I was up and moving toward her without being aware of standing, and her impish grin turned to squeals of mock terror as she pointedly ran not very far, nor very fast. I caught her wrist and yanked, and she turned and allowed herself to be pulled into my grasp. Her whole body as well as her tangled hair were soaked and freezing. As her body touched my still-hot skin I squeaked, producing an embarrassingly high-pitched noise for the third time in less than a minute. Payback was indicated.

"Oh! I've been a naughty girl!" she laughed up at me, eyes dancing with mischief, and spreading as much of her icy-cold skin and dripping hair on me as she could manage. "Brrr. I'm cold now. Warm me up."

"You bloody brat!" I sputtered, unable to adequately express my feelings of outrage. "Warm you up? Not a chance!" Now she looked uncertain, so I let her see the beginnings of a smile touch my eyes.

"This time," I said, "there won't be a warm-up."

Her eyes got suddenly large, but I didn't see them for long, as I sat abruptly back down on the soaked couch and pulled her face down over my lap. She sprawled ungracefully as she tried to recover her balance, her lovely face obscured by her mop of dark hair. I only took a second to admire the view, then set to the task of atomizing the water beaded on her ass, using the flat of my hand applied as hard as I could, over and over.

She stiffened and shrieked right away, which I could understand, as my palm was stinging madly within a few smacks. The slight layer of water amplified the sensation of the spanking, and the sound of each hard smack cracked like a muffled singletail, making my ears ring slightly. Still, fortitude is sometimes necessary in love, so I persisted.

A couple more spanks at that force and speed, and my darling Frankie began to squirm in earnest. My sweat-slicked skin made holding on to her a difficult task. I swung my right leg over both of hers and crooked my knee, leaving her draped over my left thigh, her kicking much restrained. Then I wound my left hand through her hair—the best available handle—and held tight as I continued to spank.

Damn, my hand was hurting—and so was Frankie's ass, by

the looks of her bouncing pink butt, and her hands clawing at the guesthouse rug. She was gasping some sort of unintelligible words now, but none of them resembled her safeword so I saw no reason to stop. None at all.

We continued in this way for a while, and I had a marvelous time struggling to keep Frankie in a more-or-less spankable position while keeping up the hail of stinging blows to her firm, round ass. I liked this: printing my open hand in pink over and over, and watching the prints blend together. Her hips danced to the tune of her pain, and she pushed her cunt into my knee in perfect rhythm.

Eventually my arm grew tired, so I thought of how neglected my poor sweetie must have been feeling on our overheated and undersexed holiday—and when there came a time when that didn't work to spur my flagging muscles I thought about how she'd made me squeal like a piglet. Three times. I had no real trouble after that.

Through the throb and ache in my right arm, I was painfully aware of Frankie's wiry pubes sanding smooth a spot on my thigh. Luckily she was greasing it up as well, and the heavenly scent told me it wasn't just the omnipresent layer of sweat.

Frankie cursed now, in a steady monotone, and when I let go of her hair she didn't struggle to get away, but continued cursing, eyes closed, breathing in short, sharp huffs in time with my spanks. I leaned to the right and began spanking her overhand with my left, even as I spat sloppily on the fingers of my right hand. Now my left palm stung, and I had nothing free to hold her on my lap, but she wasn't going anywhere now—not until I lifted my right leg and kicked her ankles apart, then took a split second to admire her glistening cunt, all puckered like a kiss from the pressure against my knee. I took two spit-slick fingers and pressed at her wettest spot.

I was sure this was where all the heat in the room was coming from.

Frankie moaned, then squealed again as I walloped her hard. Somewhere there, I'd buggered up the rhythm of the spanks, but nobody present seemed to mind. Something, goodness knows what, had made Frankie so wet and slick that she just swallowed my two fingers right up inside her as fast as I could shove them in. This was such an amazing thing that I had to take my fingers back so I could try it again.

The second time was as amazing as the first, so I tried it a third, then a fourth time. Repeat as necessary. We settled into a rhythm after a while. I noticed that at some point another of my fingers had crept alongside its mates, making three, and Frankie was getting hoarse from the noise she was making. I was throwing each thrust in hard—since my girl didn't have much patience or need for the soft and gentle side of fucking—and kind of pulling each stroke out along that sweet rough spot inside her cunt. Every so often I'd give her another couple of smacks on the ass instead of fucking her, which made her gasp and clench around my fingers, then work her ass impatiently, pushing her cunt onto my fingers and wiggling it around.

Rivulets of sweat streamed down my sides, across my forehead. There wasn't a hint of chill left. All the water on our skins and in our hair was like the rest of the room: blood-hot. The very air was redolent of cunt and sweat and sex, both hers and mine, and under the sounds of my own steady growl and Frankie's wails, the sloppy sound of fucking and our bodies slapping together kept a meaty accompaniment.

Now I really leaned into fucking Frankie, using my left hand to part her hot, swollen buttcheeks and pull them apart so I could get further inside her cunt. She wailed and bounced her ass back at me in time with each shove. She was thoroughly wet, yet I leaned forward and spat at the junction of her cunt and my fingers, and fucking her got even easier, slicker. So I pushed harder, really working that sweet spot inside as my darling's hoarse cries got louder and higher pitched and she ground frantically against my thigh, working her own clit that way as I fucked her fast and hard, grabbing a great big handful of her sore red ass and using it as leverage to cram more of myself inside her.

Her grasping, sucking cunt got suddenly tighter, and Frankie began trying frantically to get words out around the noises she was making. Someone else might not have been able to make it out, but I knew exactly what she was saying. Still, doesn't hurt to be clear about these things.

"What was that, baby? I couldn't quite..."

"Daddy, may I come? May I come? Daddy-may-I-come, daddy-may-I-come!" her voice grew desperate, as the magic, familiar words triggered the beginning of an explosion she didn't dare let go all the way. Her hips never ceased their frantic rhythm, and she was clenched so tight I was losing circulation in my fingers.

I spent less than a nanosecond on the thought of denying my sweet brat the release she craved, then raised my voice over her frantic mantra.

"Yes, girl. Come now." And I raked my blunt fingertips across her G-spot as hard as I could.

The last word I spoke was drowned by Frankie's shrill howl. Her cunt pulsed around me once, twice, thrice, then she spasmed even more frantically, her cunt muscles shoving me out as her legs shot out straight and a sudden hot gush of sweet, smoky-smelling girl-jizz soaked my lap.

An endless, quivering time later, she collapsed across my knee like a marionette with her strings cut. I pulled her off my knee onto the floor between my legs, and into my embrace. She smiled up at me with half-closed eyes. Her face was flushed and wet, her expression soft, and I'd never seen my baby look so beautiful. I ran my hand, all slick with juice, under her nose. Her mouth opened automatically, and I gave her a finger to suck. The first strong pull and the feel of her tongue nearly made me come right there, but I knew a better way. I leaned back and trailed my slick fingers along my belly and to my aching clit, closely followed by Frankie's greedy, sucking mouth.

Oh yeah. Maybe I *could* learn to stand the heat.

The Smell of Magic, the Thunder of Hooves

Thea Hutcheson

I was looking for some little cup hooks. She was looking for big eyebolts, right next to the decorative ones that I wanted. When I reached for them, I smelled the magic on her then, flowers and musk and excitement, all rolled up in a palatable charge that went right through me. She turned to look at me and I recognized her. Her name is Frye and she's the leather version of the charging knight from the magical land I had dreamed of since childhood.

I was kind of surprised; that wasn't the way I pictured it because the land she comes from isn't exotic in any fairy-tale way and it isn't a castle she carries you away to, it's a dungeon. I was a first-time visitor to it when I'd seen her.

Frye'd been working over a curvy blonde. The woman was bound to a St. Andrews cross and her ass was almost as red as the satin corset riding the tops of her hips. Frye had stepped in to stroke her bottom. Whatever she whispered in the bound woman's ear sent a shudder through her. My heart leapt as I wondered what she could've heard, and prayed I'd find out.

I watched her play with the blonde all night, much to my

date's irritation. Frye wore her chaps and the namesake boots matter of factly, because they suited her and what she did, which implied regular exposure over a period long enough for them to be worn in, fit to her.

Figuring out what she had been doing to wear them in taxed my meager imagination, but left me breathless. She had magic, though—there was no doubt about it—and the smell of it made me wet and hopeful. When I asked about her, people said, "Frye, she's been around forever, a wicked experienced top. She likes the new ones, the juicy ones. She likes to show them what's what. Break 'em in for the rest of us," they said, leering at each other, and me.

On her way out she'd noticed me. There was a moment of recognition and a shock when the magic made its connection between us. The smile she flashed skewered me right through my solar plexus as it made its way to my pussy. Now, in the middle of the hardware store, she looked at my coat and I knew she saw the pin from Dark House, the club where I'd seen her.

"I *thought* I'd seen you before."

The sharp stab of pleasure at her recollection nearly took my breath away. My fairy-tale knight in leathers, if not shining armor, was finally pounding down the hill for me.

"Frye," she offered her hand. "You'd be?"

"Cara, Cara Bas," I said shaking it. It was warm and strong and I imagined it against other body parts. She didn't let go of my hand and I blushed furiously.

Then her phone rang. She smiled at me with more than pleasant appreciation as she released it. "See you there sometime," she said, tapping the pin and the breast below it as she opened her phone.

And she did, fashionably mid-evening at the next party. I got to check her out first. Newly crew-cut hair accentuated the smooth planes of her face. Her leather pants sported a bulge that made my G-string wet. The white T-shirt sleeves were rolled to show off powerful arms and contrasted with her black leather vest. I smelled the magic from across the room.

I went to the buffet and picked at a few things while I waited for her to notice. It wasn't long before she was beside me. "You're here. Cara, isn't it?"

The thrill of her up close was eye candy, but her frank appraisal of the tiny mounds rising out of the top of my leather sheath told me all about the main course. She wasted no time.

"Do you want to play?"

"Yes," I said, meeting her eyes.

"Well, then, come over here on the couch and we'll talk about it." She took my arm and sat me down, setting her thigh firmly against mine. The leather of her chaps was smooth on my leg. I reveled in it until I realized she was speaking.

"Beg pardon?" I said.

She smiled wickedly. "Oh, you'll beg, but not my pardon. I said, 'Tell me about it.' Tell me the tale."

"Tale?" What was I supposed to tell her? That this maid had waited all her life to be swooped up by a knight like this and shown an exotic land?

"What do you want—what's the fantasy, the scene?"

"Oh." I wasn't sure what to ask for. I had only visited Frye's land a few times, with the dyke that started this whole quest, and the books I had read since. From the way I got so hot, I was certain now this was a land I was made to visit, maybe even move to.

I wondered what she would whisper in my ear. Then I realized I was going to find out if I just answered before she ran out of patience.

"That someone looks at me the way you do and shows me what it means," I said as steadily and sincerely as I could.

Frye paused for a moment, looking intently at me. "*Everything* it means?"

Thea Hutcheson

I looked at her beside me, solid, strong, *experienced*. She laughed as my face acknowledged the vast pit of my ignorance. I smelled the magic thick between us and straightened up. "I can use a safeword if I don't like it." I met her eyes and smiled a little. "But there's nothing in that look I don't like." I swallowed hard at my presumption. In a fairy tale, though, plucky souls could win the day *and* the heart.

She nodded. "Fair enough, and what I would expect. I'll guide you and give you an idea of what you can expect. Stake a place and I'll get my bag."

I milled for a moment, soaking in the surreal quality of it all. I was going to play with Frye, my knight in soft leather. She was going to whisper in my ear, words just for me, spoken to acknowledge my condition and what she was doing. A little twinge followed that thought when I saw her getting her bag so that she could *use* toys on me.

I thought of the blonde. I shivered and went to a suspension bridge. I liked the 360-degree effect and the way it looked like a doorway. I was ready to see where it would take me.

Frye arrived and put the bag on the bench beside her. She opened it and lifted out two cuffs, one plain, one furred.

"Do you have a preference?"

I pointed to the furred. She grinned. "A decadent little slut, eh?"

I nodded back, beaming like a headlight. She took a wrist and I pulled back a little.

"A blindfold first, please." I had learned that the first time. The black space becomes the path to an exotic land.

She shrugged and put the cuff down. I watched her face with its clean lines and hoped the flush along her cheekbone was because she wanted me.

Stepping into my space, she let me feel her warmth for a moment before placing the blindfold around my head. I closed my eyes. The sheepskin pressed softly against them. It was all about sensation now, setting me on the path to that land.

She put one arm around my waist and pressed herself against me. I groaned and breathed deeply as magic suffused the air in our space. She took my hand and wrapped the cuff around my wrist. Snugging it, she reached for the other and put it on. The bunny fur stroked my flesh deliciously, just as I'd hoped. She clipped the two together and left me to stand. A light chain clinked and a moment later she was back in front of me, reaching for my wrists. There was a sharp click when she lifted them.

She slid around me, her hands tracing my waist. Then she was on the other side, unzipping my sheath. She pulled and the lining whispered down and I stepped out of it. When she moved away I heard the ankle cuffs jingle.

She knelt and the leather of her vest rubbed smoothly against my stocking. She tightened the cuff so that the extravagant fur stroked my ankle through the hose. She positioned my legs; I heard the click of the straps and felt her test the tension. She meant to keep me where she put me. I sighed a little and she brushed up my leg, not quite to the top. When she stood I tensed my legs in the hope that she'd do it again.

She obliged, her fingers pressed against the lace G-string "I can smell you, slut. I'm gonna savor you, build it up until you're ready, and then I'll release it."

Her acknowledgment thrilled me and I thought, you smell me, I smell your magic, and away we go.

She stepped in to my side, brushing my flank with her leather-clad leg. I sucked wind when she lightly stroked the little apples of my ass. She began with strokes and pats, and finally, even though I knew what was coming, I still wasn't prepared for it when it arrived. It burned for a moment and her hand was there, rubbing, rubbing it into the most delicious warmth that somehow made a beeline straight to my clit.

"That *is* a nice ass, sweetly shaped. Good color too, which means it'll redden nicely. Wonderful, don't you think?"

"Yes, yes," I groaned, blushing outrageously because she thought so and because I discovered I loved being made to say it.

"You're a slut at heart. You just need the excuse to come out and do the deeds, and I'm happy to be your Puss in Boots. What do you think about that?"

I paused. Puss in Boots? That was a helpful cat story, a spirit guide story. But Puss helped the miller's son find a princess and a kingdom, not take the princess to the kingdom. Then her hand was on my hip and her voice whispered in my ear, every thought left my head, and my face burned like a bonfire. I answered the only words that came to mind, "Very nice, thank you,"

"Are you comfortable, do you need anything, my little marquise?" she said. "Are you ready to see what it means when I look at you?"

"Yes, please, Frye, please show me," I moaned. "Little marquise," she had called me, like "little princess" only more exotic.

"Quite heartfelt. Very well, then." She commenced spanking, giving me short volleys punctuated by soft strokes on that tender flesh, followed by increasingly bold forays to hunt around my cunt and get my clit. I was soaking when she switched to my nipples.

Oh, what a sweet land was Frye's, lying just out of sight all this time. I groaned when she unhooked the bra and my breasts swung free. They barely make cleavage but she cupped them like Fabergé eggs and nuzzled each in turn.

"Do you want me to hurt you?"

I paused. "Come on, little slut," she said slyly, "say the words, ask me to show you what it feels like to be hurt, to see where that takes you. This is part of what it means when I look at you. I want to see your nipples hard like little pegs and you arching for another pinch."

I blushed, blood racing to my face from both the shock and the remembered pleasure. "Yes," I said through air now thin and sharp. "Please, Frye, hurt me," I begged, a visitor trying desperately to do as the Romans do.

"Okay, little slut, because you beg so eloquently with your body as well as your mouth." She began to tweak my nipples, testing them to see how hard they got, how far I would squirm and still come back for more. It hurt and I cried out until it reached my pussy where it turned into a moan. The sharpness melted into a rich heat that, I swear, hummed in the center of my pussy. She alternated suckling delicately and then roughly as if she was teething. I twitched in pain, but I always came back to get more.

She stepped away and when she was back, she offered water. I realized I was thirsty and drank greedily. Blindfolded, all I had were my ears, my sense of presence, and the golden hum that resonated out from me. The resulting fire from Frye's hands arrowed deep into my soaking sex and stoked the warmth brighter each time she breached that golden space, spreading a light that showed me the landscape of her kingdom.

That meditation was broken when something whooshed loudly right beside me.

"Elk hide," she said, now running it up my back. The falls of the flogger were soft and silky—about the most decadent feeling I have ever known.

"Do you want me to flog you with it, little marquise?"

"Yes, please," I begged, curiosity warring with the dare in her voice.

She lashed me in sets of sixes and then nines, broken by strokes and brushes of her hand across my ass, a gentle touch no matter the sting preceding. I danced along a path brightly lit deeper into Frye's kingdom.

"Do you enjoy what comes of the look in my eye? Do you like what it means?"

"I do, I do, I love what you show me. It's so beautiful here." I arched to get my clit rubbed when she ran the flogger handle up between my lips. I rode it extravagantly.

"You want to come, don't you?" she asked, pressing the handle between my legs.

"Yes, I want to, I want to come," I said, greedily maneuvering that handle where it did the most good. In Frye's far-away land it became a wand, and the magic ran quicksilver into my clit. She tweaked my nipples some more and the little pinches spurred me as I rode the handle.

"That's good, but you're not ready yet. Do you want me to hurt you some more?"

"Yes, yes, please," I was suffused with the magic and the warmth of her attentions. I smiled at the way she made me light up her kingdom so I could see it.

"Very well, then, little marquise." She took away the flogger and stood on my right side, one arm down my front, the other stroking my ass. I offered it and she obliged, ramping up from comfortable to sharp. Just as I began to dislike it and contemplated saying my safeword, she rubbed those hot cheeks and petted my pussy at the same time. The resulting pleasure was so bright, the path so clear, I felt like I was floating along it.

She ramped up again and I knew she was spanking me hard, each blow palpable, shocking, and rendered totally exquisite by her fingers moving expertly through the curtains of my sex. The light blazed, everything was concentrated on her two hands.

Her fingers and hand reached a crescendo and I came, in great, shuddering gasps. I released myself into it.

There was a snap and she lowered my wrists. Slowly, methodically, she unbuckled my cuffs. After she undid the leg cuffs, she put my bra back on and slid the dress up my body, stopping to blow deeply on my pussy. I moaned, then put my hands on her head to stroke the short, straight hairs and drink in her touch.

She adjusted the sheath and finally removed the blindfold. When I opened my eyes, she was staring into them. It was a nice way to come back to this world. I contemplated her face and the perfect soul that saw me so clearly, overlaid with the warm, earthy smell of magic. I thought my heart would break with love.

She nodded and I knew she saw it too. She hugged me tightly and when she released me she stroked my cheek before leading me to a couch. She sat me down and covered me with a throw. I curled up content, but dense. She brought me water. I drank through the buzzing in my head and asked for more. She brought back fruit and cheese and another large glass of water. I was hungry and, as I ate, the buzz subsided.

After some time she asked, "Where do you live?"

"Not far," I answered, thinking how distant and alien my home and life seemed compared to the land she had showed me. "Just a couple of miles north of here."

"That's good." She paused, stroked me again. "Cara, I have to go. Things to do, people to meet. But you were just fine, a real batch of cream, and there's more to show you."

I clasped her. "Oh, please, Frye, please show me more. It was like nothing I imagined, an incredible place."

"Yeah, you went there on a rocket. You'll be a real pleasure to break in."

She picked up her bag. "Are you going to leave now or are you staying? Did you come with someone?"

I was ashamed to have not thought of it. I didn't know anyone else here. Frye was beginning to look concerned so I said, "I'll go."

"You're alone? I'll follow you home."

Now I was embarrassed. "I don't want to put you out. It really is only a couple of miles."

"I'm going north so it's not a big deal. Let's go."

I stood, we gathered our coats, and went out into the crisp fall night.

"Goodnight, little marquise Cara Bas." She smiled and kissed me on the forehead and then helped me into the car. The drive home was uneventful and she blinked her lights when she drove on. I got in the house and headed straight for bed.

I was too excited to go back to sleep, so I jilled off, replaying bits, rolling them back, freezing moments so I could explore what I'd felt. I was out like a light after I came and woke at nearly eleven, glad I'd hadn't showered so that I could awaken to her earthy magic. I jilled off again smelling it, remembering the night before.

I played the scene over and over the next day, remembering the smell of the magic and the vague, misty visions of what she might do the next time. My knight had come galloping over the rise and this plucky girl had found her very own fairy tale.

She called me a few days later. We met for coffee.

"What do you think?" Frye asked when the waitress left.

"I think I'm in love." I stroked her hand.

She looked disappointed. "You're a slut, in love with what I did, and you like the packaging."

My heart froze. She took my hand. "You knew me," I said, trying not to whine in my confusion.

"Yes, Cara, I recognize you, but you don't recognize me. I'm not the knight, you're not ready yet, you're only smelling the magic, not looking at what you see."

I stared at her. "Who are you, then?"

"Frye," she said.

"I don't remember any fairy tale with a Frye in it."

Frye looked at me very disappointed and pointed to her feet.

I sat there looking at her feet. Her boots said "Frye," just like her name. Boots. Then I remembered she called herself Puss in Boots. A magical cat? The one who won the miller's youngest son both a princess and a castle?

"But that's not the way the story goes."

"According to whose version? Don't be so anal, Cara. The details change, the story remains the same. I'm still the guide, the facilitator. And, little marquise," she said with a wicked grin, "I'm going to position you so you know what it means when the knight comes charging down the hill, looking at you the way I do."

She knows about the knight, I thought and then, stupidly, *but she's not the knight?* But what about the hardware store, hooves thundering, fully clad, and all that? I couldn't think of anything but the place she took me and the light that burned so brightly. I finally shrugged helplessly.

"And what you said before we left?" I had to try not to whine.

"I meant it," she replied. "It was an incredible scene. I've thought about it a lot the last few days. Oh, little marquise, there's much more I can show you. That's what I'm for. That's what I do. Didn't you make inquiries?"

Shame that she would think me so thoughtless made me nod fiercely. Of course I had inquired about her. Then I remembered they'd said, "Frye likes the new ones, the juicy ones. She likes to show them what's what. Break 'em in for the rest of us."

"But what you do to me...," I blurted before I could stop myself.

"Yes, little marquise Cara Bas, it is very good, isn't it? And I'm pleased to be your guide. Later on you'll remember me as the one who opened you, the one who made you ready to appreciate what your knight will do for you."

I shook my head. Frye smiled gently, patiently. "You really

are a wonder. I know—that's what I do. It's simply a matter of positioning." Her smile turned wicked and I have to admit that I blushed, thinking of my position the other night. Still.

"It's Puss in Boots?" I said, trying to make her deny it.

"I'm *not* Dyke Valiant thundering down the hill. I thought you knew when you asked to play. You asked me to show you what that look means. I thought you understood. I'm the guide, that's what I do." She paused. "You're just too caught up in the heat of the scene to see. Give it a little time. You'll see. Frye, not Valiant."

I was dismayed and crushed, but I realized that she *had* only given me what I'd asked for—to know what it means when someone looked at me like that. And I *had* learned—some of it anyway—and she was offering me more.

"Yes, you'll see. I want to show you where you're going so you're ready when the time comes." She leaned in till her mouth lay at my ear. "Which will be soon, Cara. Do you hear the thunder of the hooves coming to claim your heart and your willing body?"

I wasn't sure if I heard the hooves that carried my knight charging toward me, or heard the blood thundering in my ears. But I nodded and whispered, "Yes, Frye."

"Then patience, little marquise, I'm your Frye. I'll show you what you need to know." She patted my hand and looked at her watch.

"I've got to go." She stood and leaned over me. "I'll be at the next party. Come and I'll show you more. And you can come again too."

I grabbed her hand. "Will you fuck me next time?"

She laughed. "Greedy little slut, we'll see." She squeezed my hand and left.

Frye was right, and those thundering hooves were still a ways off, which meant she had the time to make me intimate with the meaning of that gaze and the places it would take me.

In the end, I am also a plucky slut, so I will allow Frye to position me, show me what there is to see, while I keep my ears pricked for the thunder of hooves pounding down the hill to sweep me up and away to that exotic land and the dungeon at the heart of it.

Salt
Skian McGuire

It is too hot to sleep. She doesn't want me next to her. I spread the cushion from the big papasan chair so I can lie down to sleep on the floor beside her bed like one of my own dogs. It makes me happy to think of it, imagining that I will listen to her soft breathing above me, that her hand will dangle over the edge to brush against me in the August night.

In the yellow glare of the overhead light, I take her foot to kiss it. "I am not submissive," I told her in the beginning. Without irony, she answered, "I know." I hold her foot in my hands to drink in the smell of her, and kiss it, and taste. Licking her foot, licking her lips, her ass, her belly, it is all the same to me. When she asked me what I would be to her, since I'm not a girl and I'm too old to be anybody's boy, I knew in an instant. I told her about the hounds that run through all the Irish stories, of Setanta, who became the hero Cuchulainn, King Culann's hound; and of Finn Mac Cumhaill's hounds Bran and Sceolan, who were magically transformed humans. I have felt all my life that I was more than half a dog, a human who was herself magically transformed from a hound.

Nothing could seem more natural than to become my mistress's hound. It was I who asked to wear her collar.

I am not submissive. I lick her foot for the meaty taste of her, thick in my nose and throat. I squeeze and rub and take her toes in my mouth because it makes her groan. Sucking her toes as if they were her cock makes her gasp. I would do anything for that. I swipe the flat of my tongue across her instep, smoothing the golden hair that grows so surprisingly thick there, and lap my way up the golden pelt of her legs. She does not shave, and I am grateful. I will groom her as if I were her packmate, as if she were the alpha bitch, and will lick every hair into place. I run my tongue lovingly up the hairless flesh inside her thighs, tasting salt. She says, "Oh, Goddess, yes."

I love summer. I love the sweltering air that makes her sweat and the musk of her armpit that I bury my nose in and the fine crystals, like a sheen of sparkling dust, that dry on her eyelids for me to lick off. Only a ceiling fan moves the air here, which seems thick as steam and not much cooler. I would be glad to lie on top of her, my bare torso slick, my legs suffocating in jeans I will not take off while I wear a harness, feeling the sweat burn my eyes and drip off the end of my nose as I drive my cock into her, slow and deep. I would cling to her, my breasts pressed flat against hers, while the shudders of orgasm rack her, panting *oh Goddess oh Goddess oh Goddess* as she digs her nails into the moist flesh of my upper arms, and the base of the cock banging against my pubic bone nearly makes me come.

I would. But it is too hot, she says, for me to touch her.

So I lick the hollow of her inner thigh and breathe hot breath on the crotch of her cotton panties. I tug the edge of the elastic with my tongue and gently bite her mound. My chin brushes her clit—so engorged it is visible through the opaque fabric—and she cries out. Laughing under my breath for the sheer pleasure of teasing *her*, for once, I hoist myself up on my elbows to search out the hard swell of her hip bones, kissing one then the other until I give my tongue to gentle, sunwise circles of this place she finds almost unbearably erotic.

I brush one hip bone lightly with the tips of my fingers while I lick, trailing my tongue across her belly to go from one to the other until she is moaning, her head thrown back, and she finally shoves me away. But only for an instant: she pushes her panties down and curls her legs up to pull them off. They fall by the side of the bed. She is pressing my head down wordlessly.

I bury my head between her legs, rubbing my crew cut against her sweaty crotch, rubbing her juice into my scalp, marking myself with the scent of her. She laughs and grabs, but there isn't enough hair to hold on to. I brush my nose against her honey-blonde pubic hair and pull some between my lips, tugging at her labia, and finally dart the tip of my tongue at her hard clit, a ghost touch just enough to make her shiver.

I plunge my tongue inside her then, opening her just enough to taste the tart salty juice of her cunt where it wells up. My tongue is not really long enough to fuck her with, to my lasting regret, but I try, hoping that the shallow but insistent pressure will remind her of my cock. I love to bury my cock in her, but I love this more. I run the breadth of my tongue up her pussy to her clit and lap at it, pull it between my lips and suck it like a tiny little cock, hard as a ramrod. *Oh, yes,* she tells me, *oh, that's good, oh, Goddess.* My face is wet with her juice and my own spit, wet runs down her asscheeks, wet puddles and soaks into the blue sheets. She is tart like pomegranate, her clit is a pomegranate seed between my teeth, but I do not bite. I suck her juice into my mouth and savor it. I breathe her scent into my lungs and smear it on my face. I waited for nearly a year, tasting only my own spit on plastic wrap to give her pleasure while I took in smell and touch and sound, glad of all those but longing for this, to pull her open with gentle thumbs and dip out her liquor with my tongue until I am drunk on it. Even in the stultifying city heat of this small room, my whole body shivers like a junkie who's had one delicious fix.

She had said, laughing, that she was afraid I would no longer be interested, once I got what I wanted. I had asked her how could that be, when the wanting was an ache waiting years to be satisfied?

Her clit throbs under my tongue, between my lips, my teeth scrape it and she shudders. I push her thighs apart with my elbows, letting her know that she can't close her legs. I spread her open with my thumbs, I swim in the brine of her wet cunt, my eyes stinging. Everything is sodden with sweat and juice and the humid air, we are slick with it, her thighs and my shoulders slipping against each other. She comes in small, gasping climaxes one after the other, letting me go on licking her, on and on until all at once she is nearly thrashing, chanting her small prayers as her body curls around me and her thighs clench on my head, the blood rushing in my ears like thunder.

I could lap at her all night, a restless dog, but she is satiated. I am soaked with sweat and desire, but I don't need anything more. I turn off the light. Her skin seems cool now as I kiss her good-night, letting her taste herself on me before I lower myself back to my cushion on the floor. Later, when the temperature has dropped, I may wake to find her kneeling beside me in he dark, her hand between my legs, rubbing until I want to suck her fingers into me, and I have to lift my hips for her to peel my briefs off. Later, she might fuck me in my own juice, hardly needing lube because I am still wet from memories of her, my nose buried in the lush pink folds of her cunt, her swollen clit silky-hard between my lips. Later maybe she will put her cunty fingers into my mouth to suck like a cock, to take my own taste deep into my throat and, after all of it, will straddle my face and lower herself for me to lick again.

I can't get enough, I had told her. I will never get enough. Wanting the taste of her is something that grows in me constantly, like a hunger that returns no matter how many times it's satisfied. Like something my soul needs, because at heart I am more than half a dog, my mistress's hound, and my mouth is all I have to know her with. In the heat of a summer night, I taste my own need on her, and wanting her is exactly like that—like something my body has to have, forgetting everything else until I'm crazy for it. Like something I would do anything to get. Like water in a desert. Like a craving for salt.

Hell-Bent for Leather
Rakelle Valencia

My rowels dug into her fleshy sides above her hips, leaving crimson dotted lines. I had strapped my dildo onto her, dug my spurs in, and rode hell-bent for leather.

I wanted it hard and fast. She wanted it rough. We compromised. Dusty Wranglers thrown against the wall crumpled and slid down next to the head of the motel bed to wait silently on the floor. With my boots back on and spurs buckled tight, I threw a leg over and proceeded to give her a couple of Mexican tattoos, a little something to remember me by.

My first day at the rodeo had been cursed with jitters and adrenaline rushes that wouldn't allow me to settle into my work. I'd run into the problem before, mostly from being overtired and kept propped up on caffeine while I chased the next rodeo. There was only one way to correct for it: fuck my brains out.

So, when the chute dogger sidled up to me behind the pens with obvious intent, I wrote my hotel room number on her muscular forearm...to improve my standings on the Sunday runs. Hell, she was willing to strap it on, although I could see by the blank look in her face that she'd had no experience. I'd give her that, though, and that little something else she said she was looking for.

The dong slopped in and out of my wet cunt as I sat astride. I went from a ground-covering jog into a long lope that crushed my pelvis against the base of the silicone dick and the rubber ring holding it in place. I had been so tense and pent up that it took me mere minutes to lose myself where I had wanted to. The ride broke all too soon and my spur-points stopped rolling, to dig for purchase as wave after wave paralyzed me. My slight weight collapsed onto her in a sitting slump. I hoped to be left to continue this ride from the inside, to gain a few moments of quiet.

Her hands reached for my thin waist. I smacked her searching hands away and bent forward, spurs falling from their mark. My fingers clawed in around her lower jaw. She thought I meant to kiss her full on the lips, but I wrenched her head to the side and bit her neck, hard, sucking at the clenched skin until I tasted the metallic change to its sun-kissed surface.

I ground further on the bent dick, encouraging aftershocks to rip through my thin frame. Shudders overtook me. Sweat beaded between my naked shoulder blades to form a slow run to the crack of my ass. I closed my eyes and rested my forehead, trying to listen to the distraction of the sputtering air conditioner as my wanton cunt continued to grind faster in an ever-increasing rhythm that was beginning to stiffen my thighs again.

An open hand began smacking my asscheek in a cadence devoid of conscious thought, matching a caterwauling chant for my benefit of "Oh yah, oh yah, oh baby, oh baby." Which, in another place and time, could have been good, maybe even great, but I had just met this chick. And I wasn't buying it. All I had wanted was to get off; multiple times would be a bonus.

It wasn't going to amount to anything personal, or lifelong, or with pet names for each other.

I chomped hold of her neck again to snap her skin from my teeth by pulling back while biting down. She sucked her pouty lower lip into her mouth and chewed at it with a stifled squeal that stopped the incessant monologue. "Better," I said, and ripped open the snap-fasteners of her multicolored, striped rodeo shirt that had been shelved above her luscious tits.

Her exposed nipples perked up with the air conditioner on full blast. I plucked at the points and pinged them with that action of forefinger flicking from thumb pad. "Oooh, yes," she purred. "Again."

That was about enough. I threatened her by holding up a balled boot sock and pressing a finger to her lips. She smiled through my gesture. Gagging was on her menu.

I dismounted, jerking the spur straps loose and allowing the little metal, spiked rollers to fall on the rumpled, stark sheets. With my boots kicked off, my toes hit the tight-napped carpet as if they were pounding onto cement.

"Hey, where ya going?" she asked.

Without answering I returned to the pristine, white-sheeted bed with a purple tote bag in hand. "I warned you." I ripped open a candy ring sucker, an engorged red diamond candy sitting on a plastic piece that fits on a finger, the kind bought behind the grandstands at the gay rodeo, and I stuffed it into her mouth, cherry flavored. She delighted in that idea until the duct tape ripped with a Velcro sound as I yanked it from the roll. I love duct tape.

There's the original silver tape with the strength to hold gear onto the flatbed of my truck at seventy miles per hour in a pinch, and then there is the colored kind. I chose brown; it isn't nearly as sticky or strong, but maybe I'm the only one who knows that. What this off-brand looks like is the original duct tape, even more complete with images of little yellow ducks inside the roll. It gets my point across.

I plastered a short piece across that candy, over-sized engagement ring she was sucking on, smoothing it well over each cheek. She wasn't smiling any longer, but she didn't reach to stop me.

Rescuing my strap-on and dildo from her, I then rolled her on her side and hogtied her by two bent legs at the ankles and her nearest wrist. Her ass flagged at me tauntingly. It was a plump ass, a woman's full, flat butt with generous hips. Just above her hips, dotted lines of dried blood crisscrossed almost in a star pattern but not quite. In the future I'd have to work on my spurring.

Choosing a different dick from the purple duffel, I buckled into my strap-on with the seriousness of cinching my batwing chaps for bull riding. She watched my every move. But her eyes only grew wider when I brought out a quirt.

I kneeled above her on the bed, my screaming-blue, silicone prong sticking straight out, and I laced her ass with red lines from the braided leather short-whip, a tool I'd never use on horses, as it was intended for. Five strokes and she was over the edge, ready to be fucked. A slight tear had settled in the well beside her crooked nose. And her loose hand had crept toward her crotch.

I pried one asscheek apart from the other to get a better look. She was wet. A creamy, slippery slime doused her hole, but I rolled a lubricated condom on my prick regardless.

The touch of my palm to the strips across her buttocks made the girl squirm and grunt. Her slight writhing was an invitation to my fingers. I probed her twat with three fingers, banging her G-spot. Her grunting turned to a pleading whimper. Her eyes clenched shut as her entire body moved with the pounding of my hand.

Pushing against me with all her insides, she almost expelled my demanding fingers. I shoved in harder with each thrust and absentmindedly stroked my dick. Oh, she felt good. She made me hunger to be buried inside her.

I licked my lips. I wished I could kiss hers, suck on them, but they were captured beneath the duct tape gag, a jagged line of red spittle escaping to travel down her chin and stain the white sheets.

I lined my cock up and drove into her from a kneeling position. It was on the fourth or fifth pump that she bent my shaft in half, straining against me. It was only silicone, and the eight-inch length did weaken the structure by not having the breadth. Plus, the girl had some muscles!

Back to the purple bag without delay, I doused my hand to drooling in Slippery Stuff and stroked my cock too, checking the rubber sleeve.

Her closed legs added pressure as all five of my slick fingers burrowed into her pussy. There was more resistance as the heel of my palm met her opening's ring of muscles, but she wanted it, so I waited.

She huffed and puffed through her nose, grunting deep in her throat. I moved with some slight action, encouraging her to take it all. She still wanted it. She wanted it badly enough that she strained against the hog-tie and inched her doubled body toward me.

I pushed with insistence, enough to plop through the tighter ring and let my wrist grow accustomed to her grabbing. Shoving in and out with effort, my hand truly, barely gained any distance. The movement did allow me to roll my fingers into a fist, prominent knuckles landing perfectly against her G-spot. It wasn't on purpose, but since it happened, I rocked my fist in a nod to torment her.

Instead it tormented me. Being buried in someone, flesh wrapped in flesh, the tightness, the slipperiness, the power, the warmth…it's indescribable. And it's a major turn-on. A few strokes inside her, and *I'm* ready to blow. I found myself absentmindedly stroking my dick again.

Her muscles began their play of shoving against me, and I nodded at the wrist in increasing motion to encourage this. Her grunting turned to the sound of groaning with her mouth full, which shortly turned into squealing. She bucked and humped in her restraints and gripped her eyelids shut with true tears escaping across the bridge of her nose. She was there. She was shoving me, and she was there, waiting for release, attempting to force that dam to break.

Perspiration stained my forehead even with the cooler, stale air now permeating the small room. A slow burn crept along my forearm, straining rangy muscle. She was there but she wouldn't break, or couldn't break.

My other hand choked the innocent, blue, silicone dick in an effort to balance my tiring left arm. I released the prick to slap her red-striped ass. The girl sounded out, "Ah, yah, yah, ah." Which was all well and good, but she still wouldn't go.

I had another idea.

I poked and circled her boy pussy, her asshole, to find it pliable and open. Then I rammed the lube-slicked prick into her hole.

She came. Squirting and writhing around my wrist, sopping those pristine sheets the likes to put a rust on my rowels.

I came too—alternately stiffening and jerking, giving my fist and my dick lives of their own, riding hell-bent for leather.

Casual Acquaintances
ViolyntFemme

I have never been one for anonymous sex. I am one of those queers that the second date U-Haul joke was based on. All I ever wanted was for some handsome butch to come along, sweep me straight off my high-heeled feet, and carry me away to her castle in the mountains. But I've always wanted to know the butch's name before I knew what her dick looks like, you understand? My opinion, however, was forever changed by one innocent trip to the mall.

I was browsing the lingerie section in the one of the department stores there when a low, sexy voice drew my eyes over to the men's section. The most handsome butch I had ever seen was talking to a sales clerk about a suit. You could tell the clerk was uncomfortable, by the polite yet cold tone she was using with her. About halfway through the conversation the butch looked up and caught me staring at her. A smile spread across her face as she winked at me. I became so flustered that I almost dropped the assortment of teddies and slips I was carrying over to the fitting room. Just looking at her had made me feel warm all over. My heart was beating faster, I was breathing harder, and I could feel my cunt start to get hot. I couldn't believe a stranger was having this effect on me. I tried to recover my composure by forcing myself not to look in her direction and continued toward the fitting rooms. I was just shimmying into a little black lace number when I heard a knock at the door.

"Excuse me, Ma'am?" It was her, the butch from the men's department. Her low-timbered voice sent a surge of heat straight to my clit and I had to grab the wall to keep myself upright.

"Yes?" I said, hoping my voice wasn't as shaky as my knees were.

"I was wondering if you could tell me how this suit looks on me. I think our little clerk got freaked out—she just disappeared on me."

"Well, I would love to, but I am really not dressed for it." I replied, looking down at the scrap of silk I was wearing. Even though I told myself I had no intention of showing it to her, I was secretly delighted that my underwear matched it perfectly.

"That doesn't matter. Just pop your head out. I promise I won't peek. I really need a lady's opinion on this. Please?"

I opened the door just enough to get my head through it, trying to look nonchalant about the whole thing, but I just ended up gaping at her like a teenager. She looked wonderful. The suit fit her perfectly. The cut accentuated her broad shoulders and slim hips. The black jacket contrasted nicely with her fair skin, and the shirt brought out the green in her eyes. My eyes locked on the defined bulge in her crotch for a few seconds longer than they should have. *Oh god*, I thought, *she's packing*. My heart began to race again. She ran a hand nervously through her dark hair.

"Well, is it that bad?" she asked, waiting for my opinion.

"No, it looks great on you, like it was tailored. The women will be falling at your feet if you wear that."

"Hmmm, well, I will definitely have to buy it. Do I get to see what you have on behind that door now?" she asked, her hand reaching for the top of the door.

"Um, no, thanks, though." I could feel a blush creeping up my face as I began to pull the door shut. She stepped closer to me, her finger tracing the outline of my lips.

"I saw you staring at me earlier," she said. "I also saw what you carried in here, all those lacy little underthings. Come on, be a good girl and show Daddy your pretty little outfit." Her voice carried a tone of command that my body instantly responded to, even though my brain was trying to deny it. I opened the door a bit so she could see in, and stepped back. I stood there, head down, arms at my sides, waiting for her to say something. I could feel her taking in the black lace negligee, the seamed stockings, the black lace thong and matching garter belt that I was wearing. My body felt so exposed under her gaze; it frightened and aroused me at the same time. I had never done anything like this before. Any other butch who had seen me in this state of undress had been out on several dates with me beforehand.

"You look good in that. It really accentuates your curves."

"Thank you," I said, still blushing. "Now, if you'll excuse me—" I began reaching for my dress. This had to stop right now. I was feeling uncomfortable with the hold she had developed over me in a matter of minutes. The door clicked shut behind her.

"I don't remember giving you permission to get dressed, do you?"

"I don't recall asking for—" One hand covered my mouth, the other slid down my body, heading straight for my cunt. Her body pushed mine up against the wall of the fitting room.

"I know you want this. I can see it in your eyes." A finger poked into my wet slit and I moaned into her hand. A sly smile lit up her face. "And I can feel it on my fingers. Look me in the eyes and tell me you want me to get out of here." One hand uncovered my mouth while the other one was tracing slow, insistent circles around my clit.

I looked up into her eyes with every intention of telling her to fuck off. I was not going to let this cocky butch fuck me in some dressing room. What kind of girl did she think I was, anyway? Well, apparently *I* didn't even know what kind of girl I was because instead of saying anything my mouth found hers. She pinned my arms above my head in one smooth move, her other hand never leaving my cunt.

"You didn't ask permission to do that either," she said in a low voice, her fingers snaking farther back into my cunt and entering me. "What a naughty. Little. Girl." She punctuated every word with a hard thrust into my slick hole. I was biting my own arm to keep from moaning too loud.

"You need to be taught that you don't make a move until Daddy tells you to. Understood?"

"Yes," I whispered.

"Yes, what?"

"Yes, Daddy," I whispered again.

"Good little girl, and you are going to be a quiet little girl, aren't you? You don't want someone to call the cops. Then you'll have to explain why you were in here with a stranger, letting her touch you like a little slut. You don't want that, do you?

"No, Daddy."

"But we're going to do something to ensure that you don't get too loud. Can't trust a little whore like you to do what you're told. Take off your underwear and hand it to me."

I almost protested, saying that I couldn't do this. But it would have been a lie; I wanted this more than anything I had ever wanted in my life. I wanted to be a good girl for Daddy, a good little slut. I bent over and pulled my underwear off, keeping my eyes lowered as I handed it to her. She balled it up and shoved it into my mouth, making it a very effective gag. The fact I could taste myself on it made me even hotter. She turned me around so that I was facing the wall. She pulled my legs apart and placed my arms up and out.

"You won't move unless you are told, understood?"

I nodded my head. I could feel the length and hardness of her cock pressing against the crack of my ass as she lifted my tits out of my bra. Her fingers pulled at my rock-hard nipples. My hips began to move against her.

"Don't move!" she growled into my ear. She twisted my nipples sharply and I groaned against my underwear. I could feel wetness from my cunt running down my inner thighs. She bit my shoulder, slowly working her mouth down my back. My legs were shaking but I didn't budge an inch. Her hands left my breasts and moved to my ass as she knelt behind me. I felt my asscheeks being pulled apart as her tongue caressed my asshole. A feeling of warm relaxation spread through me. I was opening to her. Soft moans came from my mouth and I pushed back into her face. I was so aroused that my cunt muscles were clenching by themselves, trying to find something to wrap around. She responded by tonguing me harder, pushing the tip of her tongue into my ass and biting the skin around my hole. I wanted to reach down and touch myself so badly, but I was afraid of the consequences if I did. I heard her zipper open and her tongue left my body. Her voice was in my ear again.

"Do you know what a little slut you look like? Your little tits hanging out of your bra, legs spread, ass in the air, and that juicy little cunt of yours just waiting to be fucked." I nodded. I knew what I looked like, and I loved it.

"Do you want me to stick my cock in that little hungry cunt? Do you want me to fuck you like a little bitch in heat?" I whimpered against the gag, and wiggled my ass, hoping she took that as a yes. I heard a tearing sound and saw a condom wrapper fall to the floor. *A good butch is always prepared*, I thought.

She moved up behind me and stuck two fingers in my cunt, testing my readiness. I immediately moved against them. Her cock quickly replaced her fingers with one hard thrust. She went in easily, the head caressing my G-spot with every stroke. I could hear the wet sucking sounds my cunt was making when she pulled out. Her hands grabbed my hips as she ground himself against me, and I could feel the teeth of her zipper pressing into my ass. I reached back to grab her hand and placed it over my mouth again. Even with the gag I didn't trust myself not to alert the entire store as to what was happening in its fitting room. My body moved against hers with abandon, not caring about being a proper lady anymore. The only thing that mattered was her, her filling me, her fucking me and making me come.

"Such a hot little cunt, such a good little girl. Move that ass for Daddy," she whispered into my ear. "I am going to come in that hot little cunt of yours, and you are going to come all over my thick cock, aren't you?" I nodded my head vigorously.

She moved my hand from its place on the wall and placed it over my swollen clit. I rubbed my clit slowly, letting the pressure build up while she pinched my tits. My ass rocked against her with more force.

"That's a good girl, come for Daddy, come all over my thick cock," she said, thrusting harder against me. "I want to feel those juices cover my cock."

She did feel those juices, too, for my orgasm was one of the hardest I've had in my life. My hips furiously hard against her, my moans loud against the gag. Through the whole thing I heard her whispering what a good girl I was into my ear.

Since that day in the store, we have hooked up a few more times. In a hotel, with her belt, she taught me the discipline I needed to learn. And I learned what a good ass fucking felt like, while sitting on her lap in the back row of an empty movie theater. I also learned that two butches can be more fun than one in my very own bedroom. But my best lesson was that anonymous sex can be hot sex, and—who knows?—she might just be the prince I've been looking for.

She, Daddy
Michelle Walsh

I felt good. I was doing my best 1930s girl that night. I had cleared a bottle of Platinum Goddess #3 and set my hair in a Jean Harlow circa 1935 style. With my red lipstick painted over with sticky gloss for added shine, I shimmied myself into a skin-tight evening gown and watched as tiny bits of glitter landed on my feet and hands. I finished myself off with an old classic, Chanel No. 5, and slipped into a pair of simple black heels that were worn down in just the right places. I caught a glimpse of myself in the mirror, smiled viciously, and as I headed toward the door, my belly was full of fire. I needed to be taken down a notch, and I would find the woman to do it if it took me all night.

The bar smelled like sweetly stale sweat, beer, and cigarettes, and the crowd stared at me as if I were an apparition. I was a girl from another era, it seemed, and the women walked by me a bit more slowly to drink me in. I watched the crowd move like a slow tide, but I didn't see her. I would know her when I saw her. I twirled my martini glass between my fingers and flinched every time I heard the front door open. As the night grew shorter and the stares from strangers grew longer and more desperate, I began to feel a bit hopeless. Sweet-faced girls continued to flirt with me and gave me goblets of wine, and while I was flattered, they weren't who I was looking for. I stretched my body against the bar and kept my eyes toward the door, waiting.

The bartender had just announced last call when *she* walked in like a slow-motion embodiment of my fantasy. She clamored into the darkness wearing a suit that fit her perfectly: pinstripes outlining her bulky arms as if they were painted on her muscles and perhaps had always been there. Judging from the thick creases in her forehead and the tiny lines in the corners of her eyes, she had to be fifteen years older than me, at least. Her hair was short, dark, and tousled, like it had been gelled then taken up in spots by the wind. She had a severe face; mean, I thought. She didn't bother to fake a smile when half the women in the bar paused in their chatter to gaze in her direction. I fell into her at once; my chest grew heavy, my forehead formed a bead of sweat, and my pussy contracted as she glanced nonchalantly in my direction. I arched my body higher against the curve of the bar, bit my bottom lip, and stared at her intently. She saw me, ignored me, and walked over to the bartender.

"Vodka. Straight up," she said abruptly, her voice masculine, loud, booming. It broke the silence in the room and seemed to echo off the bottles stacked behind the bar. Her voice made the air uncomfortable and turned every hair on my arms upright. I rubbed my eyes and looked down at my palm; it was sporting a midnight blue streak of mascara, which I rubbed absentmindedly into my palm until it became invisible. I whittled the mark away while staring intently in her direction, and though she glanced at me briefly, she maintained an air of arrogance that made my legs shake.

"You have some mascara under your eye," a girl next to

me commented, so I headed toward the bathroom. On my way, I passed her. She was leaning against the bar with one leg hoisted up on the stool in front of her, arms folded against her chest. I walked by slowly and tried to make eye contact, but she continued to ignore me.

As I approached the mirror, I saw an embarrassingly big streak of darkness under my right eye. I dabbed my finger under the running water and was wiping it away when I heard the door creak slowly open, then slam shut behind me. It was her. She stood in front of me, arms folded, face twisted into a scowl. I was completely caught off guard and didn't know what to say, so I stuttered an awkward "Hi."

"Uh–huh," she sneered. With her arms still folded tight against her chest, she looked me up and down slowly. Her eyes stalked me from head to toe and made the silence resonate while I alternated between looking nervously at the floor, the door, her shoes, and, briefly, her eyes.

"You want to get fucked, don't you?" she said sarcastically, smirking.

"Ummm. Well, I haven't really done this before, but I noticed you when you walked in and...."

"I asked you a question. It requires a yes or no answer. Do you want to get fucked?"

I thought about it for a minute and nodded my head yes. Her presence intimidated me. I felt like a child in front of her, and all the illusions and fantasies I had in my head dissolved as I stood before her. I looked down at the floor, almost afraid to look into her eyes, and nodded speechlessly, yes oh yes. I fiddled with a stray hangnail and grew embarrassed, feeling the need to escape, to turn back time and say, "No. I don't want to." But I had already said yes and now she was approaching me. Before I was aware of what was happening, she grabbed a fistful of my hair and pushed me down into a kneeling position. The cold, grainy tile of the bathroom floor scraped against my knees and although I shifted my weight, I couldn't get comfortable.

"Be a good girl and do this for Daddy," she said as she unzipped her pants to reveal a huge cock. She pushed it into my mouth and I took every inch, licking the tip first, and then swallowing its length down to the shaft. She pumped my mouth harder as I choked on her thickness, her cock turning lipstick red as she pumped it deeper and deeper into my mouth. I closed my mouth around her cock and slid my lips down to the tip, and back again. She forced her weight into me and I gagged as I heard her grunting and gasping, banging her cock against the back of my throat.

"Get up now," she said as she stuffed her cock back into her suit pants. She grabbed my back and drew me into her, grinding her hips slowly against my pussy. I could feel her cock rubbing against my clit, and my cunt tried to swallow it through our clothes. She gripped me tightly and I noticed that she was much stronger than me. I tried to struggle against her weight, but she overpowered me. My pussy grew wet as she thrust her heavy body into mine. My legs were shaking and I felt what I could only describe as ecstatic panic. I was terrified, though I wanted her inside me.

"Let's get out of here," she said as she grabbed my hand, leading me out of the bathroom and through the crowded bar. Everyone stared, and some women even gasped as if they were afraid for me. She opened the door of an old Buick and sat me down in the passenger seat. She didn't say a word the whole time we drove, and my heart raced with tinges of both fear and anticipation. When we finally arrived at our destination, she parked the car, reached into the backseat, and pulled out a strip of black cloth. Grabbing me by the neck, she tied the cloth around my eyes. "Can you see anything?" she asked. I couldn't see a thing and I told her so. I heard my passenger door open and felt a cool gust of wind, then her warm hand wrapped tightly around the base of my neck. She guided me up at least five flights of stairs this way, until I heard a door open and felt carpet beneath my feet.

"If I take this blindfold off, are you going to be a good girl and do whatever Daddy tells you to do?"

"Yes, I will. I promise," I said quietly. She grabbed me from behind, her left arm wrapped around my hips, and I could feel her warm breath on my neck as she tore the blindfold from me in one long stroke.

"Good. Now I want you to lift your dress up and bend over that chair for me." She pointed to a small wooden folding chair at the kitchen table.

Her hands were undoing her belt buckle as she ordered me to the chair. My pussy clenched again and I could feel my own wetness seeping between my thighs, sticking to my dress. She slipped the belt out from its belt loops and held it in front of me. I could smell and taste its heavy leather from where I stood. Her eyes looked infuriated and filled with fire as I felt a stream of real fear sweep through me.

"Over the chair, I said. I want to see your ass over that chair right now!" she cried, her voice booming.

I lifted my dress and bent over the cold wooden chair. She pulled my shoes off and I heard them fall softly in the distance, as if she had thrown them across the room. Her hand rubbed my ass, and for a moment it felt comforting. I felt her bunch my panties in her hand, pulling them tight between my asscheeks, and in one quick yank she ripped them from around me. "Ouch!" I yelled as my pussy stung as if from a rope burn and my skin flinched beneath me.

"Don't ever say ouch again," she warned as she cleared her throat and glided the leather belt slowly back and forth across my bare ass. The corners of the chair were digging into my stomach and my knees were hurting from trying to balance my body. It seemed like an hour before she raised the belt high above her head and slammed it down on my ass with tremendous force. My whole body stung and my eyes began to water, but my pussy was begging for her to do it again. She struck my ass three more times, each lash growing harder than the first. My body was stinging as I choked back the urge to cry.

"Beg me to whip your ass. Beg Daddy to whip your ass again!" Her voice seemed to shake the room.

"Please whip my ass, Daddy," I said in a choking voice. I could hardly get the words out.

"I didn't hear you, little girl! You want to try that again? You don't want to piss me the fuck off right now, do you?" I heard her shoes creak on the floor behind me.

"Please whip my ass, Daddy. I want you to hurt me, Daddy. I've been very bad," I yelled. My pussy was contracting and I could feel it growing wetter with each slap of the heavy leather.

She brought the belt down on me ten more times, and with each lash I heard her grunt in satisfaction. My ass was burning and as I fought back the tears all I could think about was having her huge cock inside me. As I lay bent over the chair, she walked around in front of me and pulled up another chair. She put the belt back around her waist, sat down on the chair, and said, "Don't you even *think* of moving off that chair." Her voice was gravelly and she was slightly out of breath. I watched her reach into her suit pocket to pull out a long, thick cigar. She lit the tip, put it to her lips, and stretched back in her seat with her legs splayed out in front of me. She took long drags of the cigar and stared at me intently as I looked up at her. My body was uncomfortable and I kept shifting my weight.

"Put your ass higher in the air!" she demanded and I arched my back as high as it could go until my stomach was no longer touching the chair. "Daddy wants to look at you for a little while." She exhaled as she began to stroke her cock on the outside of her pants. I fought to keep my balance as I lifted my ass as high as possible. I was afraid I was going to slide off the chair and I laughed weakly, "I'm going to fall off the chair!"

"Are you laughing? You think this is fucking funny? I don't care if you're uncomfortable. I want you to stay draped over that chair until I'm done smoking."

"I'm sorry, Daddy."

"Yeah. You're gonna be goddamn sorry if you don't shut your mouth." She grabbed my face with her left hand and squeezed my jaw till I thought it was going to snap, and then she exhaled a cloud of smoke into my face. She cleared her throat and sat back, blowing heavy clouds of cigar smoke in my direction, looking me up and down as she ran her hand slowly along the thick outline of her cock. My whole body was aching as I fought to stay in the position. Just when I felt my body on the verge of collapse, she stomped the cigar stub out in an ashtray on the kitchen table. She was turned away from me as she extinguished the flame and growled, "Get up off that chair and follow me." I pulled my body into a standing position and though I ached everywhere, I ached even more to know what she would do next. I followed her down the long hallway that led to a bedroom and when she opened the door, I noticed it smelled like leather. The door slammed shut behind us as she pushed me down on the bed and handed me a tissue.

"Wipe that goddamn lipstick off your face right now. I want you to suck my cock again and I don't want that shit all over me."

"Yes, Daddy. I'm sorry."

"Don't you know only big girls get to wear lipstick, anyway? Now wipe that shit off fast and get on your knees!"

I scrubbed my lipstick off with a tissue and dropped to my knees in front of her. Her cock was already sticking out of her pants and my mouth was starving for it. I sucked her cock hard as her hips pumped it in and out of my mouth. I could smell the cigar smoke clinging to her pants and felt sweat forming between her thighs. "Good girl," she said, over and over again, as I sucked her. My throat was hurting from her sharp thrusts and my pussy was dripping down my inner thighs. "Get that dick nice and wet because I am going to fuck the shit out of you in two seconds. You want Daddy to fuck you?"

"Yes, Daddy, please fuck me. Please!" I murmured as I sucked harder. My own saliva was dripping down my chin and her cock was so wet that it kept slipping out of my mouth. I could feel my pussy contracting, craving her big cock inside me. She pulled me by my hair into an upright position and threw me down on the bed, ripping my dress in half along the side seam. She climbed on top of me and her weight pressed me down into the bed. I grabbed her arms; they were hard muscle and I couldn't move an inch beneath her.

"Is my little girl cunt hungry?"

"Yes, Daddy. My cunt is hungry for you. Please fuck me hard."

Her cock fought to get inside me and she began to thrust into me, slowly at first, then harder and faster until the room began to spin. I was pinned beneath her like an insect and I couldn't move, so I lay back and held onto her neck while her cock plowed me.

"You like that, sweetheart?"

"Ya. Yesss...Dad...dy."

"That's a good girl."

As she pumped me harder, she took her index finger and swirled it around the inside of my mouth. I bit it gently and she slapped me hard in the face. My cheek stung and grew hot as she pulled her cock out of me and walked to the other side of the room to light a cigarette. Her face was infuriated and sharp.

"Sit up!" She exhaled. "Did I tell you to do that?"

"No. I'm sorry."

"I'll teach you to fuck with me. Who's running the show here, little girl?"

"You are, Daddy. I'm sorry. I was just kidding."

"Kidding? You are such a bad girl. Just for that I'm going to take your ass." She paused. "Have you ever had a cock up your ass, honey?"

"No, Daddy. Please don't hurt me, though. It might hurt because I haven't done it before."

"It might hurt a little bit, but it makes Daddy really hard to think about slamming your virgin ass. You want to make Daddy happy, don't you?"

"Yes, I do. OK, Daddy."

"Now get down on all fours!" she boomed as she approached the bed again. I pulled myself up, rolled over, and held my body up for her. I heard her spit and then felt her calloused fingers massaging my ass with the wetness. Before I knew what was happening, she was inside me. It hurt at first, and then I could feel her cock hitting my pussy. My body was surging and pulsating like electricity as she pumped in and out of me. "Oh, fuck!" I yelled.

"Don't swear in front of your Daddy unless he tells you to, girl. I'm going to pound your ass harder for that one," she said as she slammed into me with all her weight. "Oh, yeah, you've got a tight little virgin ass." The weight of her thrusts pushed me halfway across the bed, but she pulled me back toward her and held onto a fistful of my hair. I heard her moaning and gasping for breath as her hand slid beneath her cock and began massaging her clit. I could hear her wetness, and mine, sloshing beneath our gasps and as I was about to explode she cried, "That's a good girl. Come for Daddy. Come for Daddy!" My body convulsed and a stream of wetness shot out of my pussy. I collapsed on the bed beneath her and she climbed on top of my face, moved her thick cock to the side, and shoved her pussy into my mouth. "Let's see how my little girl eats cunt," she whispered as I craned my neck to bury my tongue deep inside her. She was sopping wet and I dug my tongue into her clit, flicking it back and forth along her hardness.

"Eat it up, little girl. Oh yeah, that's my girl!"

My face was dripping wet as I chewed and sucked her clit. She bucked her hips into me and began to ride my face. I teased her ass with my tongue for a while, then dove back into her clit, rolling and flicking along the surface. She rubbed her pussy faster and faster over my mouth, then I heard her inhale deeply and a stream of wetness shot out of her, drenching my face and hair. She got up from my face and walked across the room. When I sat up I felt her juices running down my neck. I absently wiped the underside of my chin and her eyes flashed at me.

"What the fuck are you doing?"

"Nothing. What do you mean?"

"What do I mean? I just caught you wiping Daddy's cum off your face! Did I tell you to do that?" she shouted.

"No. I'm sorry, Daddy. I didn't mean anything by it."

"Yeah. OK. You know what I think? I think you need to be taught a hard lesson. I didn't think I would have to do this with you, but apparently you're full of yourself and need to learn a little humility. Now come with me into the bathroom."

She grabbed my arm tightly and led me into the bathroom where she instructed me to get into the empty bathtub. I did as I was told, but my heart was racing with both fear and excitement. "Keep your eyes on me," she said. "I want you to look up at me and to not take your eyes off me, no matter what happens. Understand?"

"Yes, Daddy. I understand."

Michelle Walsh

She stood with one foot on the floor outside the bathtub while the other was propped against the bathtub ledge behind my head. She arched her hips so that her pussy was right in front of my face, then she grabbed my hair and forced my head even closer to her.

"Now, Daddy needs to take a piss, and since you're such a fucking prima donna, I am going to piss all over your pretty little face." My pussy contracted and grew wet again but I kept my eyes on her, as she demanded.

"Now tell me that you want it, little girl."

"Piss all over me, Daddy. I deserve it. I'll take it for you."

She moved her pussy even closer to my lips and unleashed a heavy stream of hot wetness all over my face and hair. It dripped down my chest and made my nipples erect, then trickled down to my pussy and legs. I kept my eyes fastened on hers and she stared at me intently the whole time until she was drained and said, "Good girl. Now lick my pussy clean and then you can clean yourself up." My mouth was hungry for her again and I lapped at her pussy like a hungry animal until the only wetness left on her was from my tongue. Then she turned the shower on and she told me to stand up under the spray of warm water while she wiped me down with a red facecloth. As I turned to rinse my hair, she slipped three fingers inside me and pumped my pussy hard. "This is for being so good," she grunted, and I came all over her hand instantly.

I followed her back into the bedroom where she began to get dressed, while one hand opened a dresser drawer and pulled out a large white men's dress shirt. She tossed it in my direction. "You'll need this, since your little dress is torn to shreds."

I whispered, "Thank you, Daddy." I put the shirt on and it fell past my knees. The sleeves hung over my hands so I wore it like a dress.

150

"I need to get up early tomorrow, sweetheart. Do you need a ride home?"

"Yes, please."

I got up from the bed and followed her down the hallway and to the front door. As we walked toward the car, it began to snow. The chill bit my face and hands as I wrapped the shirt tighter around my body. She asked me if I was cold and I told her I was freezing so she took off her coat and wrapped it around me. It smelled like a mixture of cologne, smoke, and leather. When we got to my apartment she parked the car and walked around to the passenger side and opened the door. As I exited, she took her right hand and squeezed my neck tightly.

"Are you going to be a good girl while I'm away?"

"Yes, Daddy. When will I see you again?"

"Here's my phone number." She slipped a small strip of paper into my hand. "I want you to call me on Tuesday and I'll come pick you up. Remember, your pussy belongs to Daddy now, and I don't want anyone else touching it between now and then. Do you understand?"

"My pussy is yours from now on, Daddy," I replied. "I promise, it's all yours."

"I'm glad you know that, honey, because if I even suspect that you lied to me I will put you over that chair again. Do you understand?"

"Yes." I smiled and looked up at her. She kissed my forehead and headed toward the car.

Tuesday was three days away, and my body convulsed as I counted the days until I would see her again.

The Heat and the Cool
María Helena Dolan

The sun is brutal. It's multitasking—hammering and sizzling my hard-hatted head. That damn hard plastic helmet acts like a crown of thorns, pushing into my scalp—a scalp with aggravated pores sluicing sweat out and down while the hair sticks to my head like wet leaves.

This job has made me get neoprene to protect every conceivable joint in my body, and today I'm wearing the wrist wrap. Right now, my wrist feels like meat encased in foil, slathered with barbecue sauce and set out on the goddamn grill.

I can sure feel the freakin' sweat that started out at my neck, took its time getting down between the shoulder blades, then picked up speed running down my spinal column until it pools where the shirt, pants, and underwear meet, soaking me through.

The sun on my black boots makes my feet want to holler for heat relief. I can about wring out the socks and the pads. The garish safety vest is sticking to me, pinioned by those solar flares, too, adding to the fun. With no breeze to move it off my body, the only momentary relief comes when I swing my arm away for half a second.

Then there's sweat from my armpits, running in rivulets and collecting in giant full moons under my arms and spreading all through my bra, soaking it unmercifully. That underarm sweat even slides down the inside of my arms, the T-shirt not able to stop it from running down to my fingers. I can shake them and get drops of sweat to spring off me.

And don't forget the sweat pooling under my eyes, which threatens to swamp the too-little-sleep bags there, and contributes to the runoff over my lip. The salt stings my eyes and just slithers down the sides of my face, adding to the heat and the misery.

I ask myself, is this any way to make a living? Under the sun with the boys out on the tracks? Sure, rail needs replacing. But why in hell am *I* doing it?

Well, I'm not actually doing it at the moment. I'm waiting for Rerun to bring the right toolbox from the truck—that fool got his name from always having to do shit over again. So I and the rest of the crew are standing around, feeling fairly wretched and waiting for the signal so we can use the hi-rail vehicle's crane to lift rail onto the trackway and set it down into place.

Fuck this. I want cool. I want last night. I want Ginni and the waterbed. Standing under the sun right now, sweating my tits off, that seems so long ago....

I'd taken my shower, washing off the track dust and the day's aches, hair no longer plastered to my head, skin no longer laced in tracks alternating sweat, ballast dust, and Georgia clay.

A cold white wine and my baby both calm me down. After dinner, which is salad and cold cuts, we go to bed. It's so great that the heater for the water bed broke! Now we can lie on the bed with just a sheet, and feel the heat being sucked right out of us. Ah, bliss! Just lying there cooling, my fingertip on her thigh for contact, the sun and the day fading off into the distance, a little music playing, the light down low. Coolness; the air conditioning, the waterbed, and her. A perfect moment.

I don't want to move. I just want to breathe and sigh and stretch out and uncoil and feel the coolness. This is bliss. Shoot me while I'm happy.

But of course I can't just lie there next to her forever without wanting to touch her. The fingertip on her body becomes four fingertips, then a palm gliding along her thigh, working slowly up her side and back down again.

She turns her head to me, opens that sweet mouth, and asks, "What're you doing?"

A grin comes up on me kind of slow, and I just keep on doing it, up and down, flesh to flesh, fingertips tracing little circles on smooth skin.

"I thought you were too hot."

True, I'd said it, maybe even meant it for a minute. Like in the Cole Porter song, "It's too darn hot!" But that was then, and now there's skin to skin and coolness.

Still grinning, I allow, "No, baby, you're the hot one."

She snorts at this, but doesn't pull away. In fact, her nipple stiffens, pointing upward, which means I have to trace it with a fingertip too.

"You tease."

"You know I'm gonna deliver the goods. It just takes a while."

"'Deliver the goods?'" she repeats, making it sound illegal or improbable or something.

"Yes'm, just like UPS," I say as I take her nipple in my mouth.

"Mmm, this isn't the usual package," she says, her voice a sly smile.

"Very special delivery, just for you," I say as I move on up to her neck, which seems to need kissing, and then on up to her mouth, which definitely needs kissing. Her own kiss is soft and just the right mixture of full lips and full tongue, mine sliding over hers and hers sliding over mine, again and again, little thrills passing between us, electric tendrils with shocks extending from mouth to breasts to cunts.

I slip one hand under her neck, and put the other onto her breast, kneading the nipple. She reaches for mine, finds it, and we both work each other. This feels good, this feels right, this feels sharp and soft and warm and cool at the same time.

I move my hand lower, running one of my nails down her ribs and onto her stomach, which causes her to shiver. She still has my breast and we're still kissing, but now the focus begins to shift as my hand reaches to where thigh meets belly, and wanders over to her cunt.

Using the palm of my hand, I rub lightly against her, and her hips begin to move, just a little. "Pull yourself up," she commands softly, and I do, lifting myself from behind her neck, settling a little higher beside her, one of my legs lying on top of one of hers. I start to rub harder with my hand, and she reaches down toward my pussy, but can't slip past the press of our bodies.

"I can't reach you. I hate that," she complains, and I shift onto my side so she can. She lets her hand start on me, as I continue to rub in small circles against her fleshy rise. She runs her finger over the place where my mound begins, which shocks and delights, as I know I shock and delight her.

"Oh yeah, baby, right there, like that," I call. She has two fingers now, spread on either side of my clit, moving up and down. I do the same on hers, and her hips rock back and forth, keeping time in a rhythm we both know in our bones.

I go down a little lower, feeling the fullness of her erection and rubbing up and down the whole clit. Her hand is squeezed between our bodies, but she keeps up a steady rhythm, all up and down and over me.

I reach down further, finding the wet place and putting a finger in, while rocking against her clit with the heel of my hand. She shudders and shakes all the more.

I get to my knees, and ease the finger out of her.

"Oh, I hate that," she complains.

"Well, you'll like *this*," I counter as I flip in the other direction, my head down to her cunt, my own pussy within reach of her mouth. Greedily, we both set to work, I on top, she spread out beneath me. Her tongue is a natural wonder, working up and down and over and around. It never stops moving, stays right on me as I start to pulse. Man, she's good, and I start to get all heated up again, and have to work to concentrate on what I'm doing. I wrap my tongue around her clit as if I'm eating the most succulent treat on earth, which I am. I lick and lick, bobbing my head like a cat over a saucer of heavy cream.

She's making me sweat and squirm and press down harder, making heat rise in a wonderful way, all while I'm giving it to her and giving it to her. I feel her rolling under me, pushing up against my face, trying to get every bit that I'm giving.

My whole middle is on fire, throbbing relentlessly, my clit so stiff it's about to burst. I bear down harder, I'm so close, while my tongue keeps on, and I don't know who's going to blow first, me or her.

I hit that sweet spot and I grind my cunt into her, grind for all I'm worth, grind until I lose my mind, a sound coming out of me that's a cry and a sob and a groan, and I aim it right into her pussy and she's there, she's right there, and then she trips over the edge, letting it all loose, thrashing all around, screaming into me, her cunt reverberating and sending rings of energy outward while her silky essence bathes my face.

It takes a while to understand that we've stopped moving.

It takes another while to get air back into our bodies. I roll off her, still gasping. She crawls toward me and wraps her arms around me. "I love you," she says as she looks into my eyes. It's so naked and so raw and so true, I can only return her gaze and say, "I love you, too."

Heart to heart, hip to hip, face to face, we lie together as the bed sucks the warmth from our bodies, and we're simply glad to be able to lie here together. This is soft and cool and perfect, as I pull the soft cotton sheet over us.

Yeah, that was last night. Tonight too, if I'm lucky. No more broiling with the boys under the hot sun. Just the cool and the dark and me and her, anticipation sharp as I wipe sweat off me and hit the auxiliary control switch to get the rail car rolling again.

Game, Set, and Match
Cheyenne Blue

The barbecue at my brother's house promised to be the usual mundane crowd of jawing suburbanites, and I hadn't wanted to go. He and his equally dull wife lived in one of Melbourne's most mind-numbing suburbs, and any gathering they hosted was a boring cacophony of accountants, teachers, and housewives all chattering on about their kids. Not my scene at all. If it were up to me, I'd have spent my Sunday afternoon—the hottest day of the Melbourne summer so far— in my air-conditioned apartment exploring the possibilities of my new vibrator. But I had to go. It was his birthday and I'd promised.

I arrived late, grabbed a beer, and looked around. Same old, same old. I made a mental note of the whereabouts of a few people I wanted to avoid, and went to sit in a quiet corner, waiting until I could grab my brother, give him his present, and get the hell out of there. Even in the shade of a large wattle, the sweat rolled off me in waves, soaking though my singlet and into the waistband of my shorts. With nothing better to do, I idly watched the guests.

I saw her almost immediately, and my gaydar gave a little ping. Hell, who am I kidding—it leaped off the scale. I looked closer. She was younger than I was, maybe in her early twenties, and the sort of cool blonde preppy kid I normally avoid. She was wearing tennis whites—a fresh, newly pressed skirt and a sort of cute, bobsy little top. Her hair was pulled off her neck into a jaunty ponytail. I watched her chat with my niece's kindergarten teacher, a desultory conversation that had her eyes flitting around the backyard looking for escape.

The second time her eyes swept over me, I stared back. Her gaze moved on, then snapped back as if it were on elastic. I chugged my beer, threw the can into my sis-in-law's banked rows of flowers, and waited for her to approach.

It took, oh, two point six minutes. I had closed my eyes, and was jerked up in my seat by the feel of an icy-cold tinnie rolling around the back of my neck.

"Need a beer?" she asked.

She moved in front of me, and her crotch was level with my eyes. The short tennis skirt swayed as she shifted, and her lean brown legs had the sort of glorious bowline to the inner thigh that I love. Curved, and hollow. It always makes me want to rest my cheek there, and savor the taste of things to come, and this was no exception. I could see downy blonde hairs on her thigh, so fine they could be cobwebs.

"Yeah, thanks." I dragged my gaze from her legs and accepted the beer.

"I'm Pippa." She squatted down on the grass in front of me, and I could see her panties. White, of course, to go with the tennis outfit. I could smell trouble, there in the salty waves coming off her cunt.

"Excuse the clothes," she continued. "I live next door, and I was going to play a set with my sister, but she changed her mind when she saw the free beer here."

"You have a court next door?" My interest was roused.

Tennis is my game too. I like the competition, the combination of skill, force, and of course the women in shorts. Martina Navratilova got a lot of dykes into the game, and I'm no exception.

"I do. Not a very good one, but I don't care. I like a game."

"Me too." I chugged my beer, and stood. "Wanna play?"

She caught my double meaning, no doubt about that, but she didn't hesitate. Her eyes raked me from top to toe, taking in the singlet and baggy shorts. "You got shoes?"

"In the car. I'll get them."

"That house there," she said, jerking a thumb. "The court is at the back, behind the hedge. Very private, you can't see it from the road, or from here."

Her meaning was obvious, and a tingle of arousal ran from my nipples to my cunt, as surely as if they were connected by a cord.

"Five minutes."

When I found the court, she was already there, practicing her serve. I watched for a moment, studying her long, loose swing, and the way she threw the ball high, before pounding down on top of it. She was good. I picked up the spare racket leaning against the chair, walked to the opposite end, and bounced experimentally on the balls of my feet. Pippa inclined her head and batted a slow one at me. I corrected my stance and drove back a forehand down the tramlines. For a few minutes we rallied to and fro, warming up. She was a club player, that was obvious; good control and heavy topspin. Not too much power behind it. I was more rough and ready, somewhat wilder, but I had greater strength, and erratic flashes of brilliance.

We tossed for serve and she won. I nearly missed her first ball—I was watching how her skirt flipped up, showing her panties as she smashed down on the ball. My return went wide. Fifteen-love. I concentrated on the second point, and we fought a long rally. Her long brown legs flashed around, and her breasts jiggled with the force of her groundstrokes. A distraction for sure, but I held my own, making her run. Fifteen-all.

For the next twenty minutes, we played with heavy concentration. I summoned the steel of my idol, Martina, and fought every point doggedly, my flashes of luck compensating for my unpredictable backhand. The sweat rolled, and my hair clung to my neck in damp spikes, but I kept fighting.

She was three-two up, and we were changing ends when I made my move. She handed me the water bottle, but instead of taking it, I grasped her wrist and pulled her closer, enough that I could see her dusky nipples underneath the white top.

Her smile was feline. "I didn't think you really wanted to play tennis."

In answer, I wrapped my arm around her neck, bringing her close. I could see the sheen of dampness on her cheeks, her parted lips, before I closed the gap and kissed her. The day may have been hot already, but when her lips touched mine, the temperature shot up by another few degrees. Her hands—tiny hands, I noticed now—anchored my head and our mouths crashed together, opening, tongues tangling.

Liquid her mouth, and instantly liquid my cunt. Our hands were exploring: her back, my shoulder, her waist, my breast. I dropped my head, and sought the curve of her neck and shoulder, pushing my face into the muscle, smelling fresh sweat and sunshine. My tongue lapped at her sun-warmed skin, salty like the sea.

Pippa tilted her head, letting me explore, encouraging me with small mumbles of pleasure. Her scent rolled off her, intoxicatingly female. I fancied I could smell her salty cunt, curling through the humid area.

The sun burned hot on the back of my neck, and the sweat

ran in runnels down my thighs. My panties were damp, but that wasn't only the temperature. Taking my hand, Pippa led me beyond the baseline to where the wattles dropped golden flower globes onto the ground. Here the hardcourt ended and the grass began, long grass, uncut, and starting to wither with the fierceness of the Australian summer.

With a long look, she grasped the hem of her top with both hands and pulled it over her head. A plain white cotton bra hid firm breasts, heavy with wide dark nipples. I touched one with my fingertip, watched it instantly tighten. Her skirt dropped away, leaving her in those ridiculously frilly tennis panties.

Swiftly, I stripped off my own damp singlet, and let my shorts drop to the ground. I never wear a bra—don't need one with my boyish chest—and my panties were plain, serviceable cotton. I kicked my clothes away.

She reached for me at the same instant as my hands sought her body. We sank to the ground, and my face was in her breasts, palming her nipple, and biting gently on its partner. I had expected her to be more passive, more diffident in her approach to sex. The ponytail, the whole tennis thing had led me to expect that I would be the aggressor. But Pippa was fighting for the upper hand, trying to push me over onto my back so that she could feel my breasts.

For a moment, I gave way, and abruptly I found myself on my back with her astride me. Our panties touched and our thighs rubbed together. My palms smoothed her inner thighs, finding the curve I love so well. Her fingers rubbed my nipples and I sighed in pleasure, closing my eyes against the bright sunlight that filtered through the trees. When her hand crept under my panties, I raised my hips, encouraging her to remove them. She took the hint, and immediately her fingers were there, sliding over the lips, then dipping inside. Pippa shifted, lying between my spread thighs. One finger, two, then three, slipping slowly in and out, sliding easily in the moisture, curling around, pressing up, stretching me, finding my G-spot with easy skill. She pistoned fast, fucking me with her small hand, a welcome penetration. When her thumb passed over my clit, the spasms started, intensified, and burst in a rolling golden wave of pleasure. My back arched from the ground and my mouth opened in a soundless scream.

When the spasms eased, I became aware of our surroundings, the dry grass stalks in my back, the shrill of the cicadas. Pippa raised up, and pressed her fingers to my lips, forcing me to taste my juices. I allowed it for a minute, while my breathing slowed, steadied, and then I pushed her hand away.

My turn.

Still on my back, I encouraged her forward, guiding her thighs so that they settled on either side of my head. Turning, I pressed a kiss against their lean curve. Her panties were gone, kicked away to lie in the grass. Instead, there was her bare pussy inches from my mouth, covered with downy blonde hair, musky with the scent of summer. I learned her with my fingertips, tracing the lines of her lips, feeling the texture of her moisture. And then, when the longing became too much, I tasted *her,* savoring the starburst of her cunt on my tongue. I was gentler than she had been; I lapped with short, gentle strokes, then pushed my tongue in deep, seeking paradise.

Pippa's thighs clenched about my head, clamping on my ears so much that the pressure created an artificial sea-murmur in my ears. Her hair had worked loose from the ponytail, and curled in damp tendrils against her neck. But I didn't let her come; as she worked up to her peak, as her moisture flowed freely over my mouth and chin, I eased back, and pushed her off my face, an abrupt motion that had her sprawling in the grass. She stared up at me, the sex-flush spreading down over her pale breasts.

I parted her legs and reached for the tennis racket. The

handle was worn smooth from years of sweat and firm grip, and it was fat and hard. I eased it into her cunt, letting her relax around the intrusion. Then, letting it rest, I put my mouth back down to her snatch again. This time, I kept going, tonguing her hard, lashing her shivering clit with long, wet strokes. When she came, the racket quivered in her cunt, trembling against the side of my face.

I pulled it out, and handed it to her. Her fingers closed around the grip, and she mimed an imaginary backhand slice.

"I think this racket's just played its best match," she murmured.

Her sleepy, cat-slit eyes told it all. I rested my head down again onto her thigh, and let my fingers tangle in her soft pubes.

My words vibrated against her skin. "Fancy a rematch sometime?"

Porta-Potty Passion
Sarah B. Wiseman

Most days, I wouldn't consider the porta-potty on my work-site a good place for a quickie. Usually, all I feel about it is grateful that it's there to give me a few minutes of refuge from long days of lifting, measuring, cutting, and nailing into place, two-by-four after two-by-four. No, I wouldn't have thought it would be the ideal spot for a little one-on-one. But where did I find myself, week before last, in the middle of a sweltering August afternoon?

You betcha: rocking away in that damn porta-potty.

Nobody particularly noticed when she walked onto the site that day. And if they did see someone step into the porta-potty, they probably assumed it was a teenage boy from the high school across the road.

I was pounding a joist when I noticed her walking up the gravel road. First off I couldn't tell, but it didn't take long before my gaydar kicked in and I got a hint of dyke in her boy swagger. She looked up to me on the second floor where I was framing as she walked toward the john and the first thing I thought was, *Man, she has balls.* And then, *What a gorgeous smile*. I followed her with my eyes, careful not to draw attention from the guys on my crew, and watched the blue door bang shut behind her and the green VACANT sign shift to a red OCCUPIED.

I continued to pound spikes into the joist I was working on, and when I looked up again, I saw the porta-potty sign reading VACANT.

I looked around the site and didn't see her. I turned to my crew to see if they had taken notice of the hot bulldyke in the porta-potty and this hot bulldyke's reaction to her. Seeing that they were indeed oblivious, I made my way down the ground ladder and across the street to the porta-potty.

I opened the door to find a half startled, half expectant, fat butch dyke sitting on the lid of the can, her legs planted wide. I locked the door behind me.

"Hey," I said, putting my hard hat on the floor and running my fingers through my short sweaty hair. She wore a baseball hat backward.

"Hey," she laughed deeply. "My name's Al." She sounded calmer and cooler than I felt.

I took a small step that put me between her legs.

"Joe," I said and put my hand against the back wall beside her head.

"Joe Blow?" she asked, turning her hat around, brim to the front. She didn't smile. I could tell she was twice as cocky and just as easy as I was.

I laughed and took her question as an invitation. I bent down so our faces were a few inches apart.

"So you want this?" I said. Meaning, a good fuck in the sky-blue john on a hot afternoon in the middle of August.

I put my hand on the seat right between her thighs and felt something hard nudge my wrist through her pants. Apparently this wasn't some random visit to the construction site on her part. Did she think someone would be here to take advantage of this? Maybe she *was* a teenager from the high school across the road.

"Fuckin' right," Al said, standing up.

She put her arm around the back of my neck, grabbed my hair, and pulled me to her. I kissed her softly at first and then hard. She kissed me even harder, and pushed me against the blue door. She panted hard, biting and pulling at my lips. My hand squeezed her thigh, working its way up, while she clutched at my shoulders and moved her hands around my waist, pulling up the Midnight Oil shirt on my back.

Sweat slid down the crack of my ass. It made me feel like fucking. I unzipped her cargos and slid my hand in to find briefs and sticky thighs. Her hand snuck under my bra to my hard nipple and I put my fingers through the cock hole of her briefs.

Packing, indeed. She was sporting a good-sized rod. One to make all the boys on site shrivel a bit under their toolbelts. I took a minute to swing my own toolbelt from the front to the back. I was going to need room for this one.

Getting my drift, with one cocky motion, Al loosened her pants and slipped them down to the ground. Her dick wobbled in its straps. The smell of her cunt in the heat of the day traveled quickly, even through the stench of the toilet. I pushed her back down onto the seat of the john and pulled my own jeans down far enough so I could straddle her. My hammer felt cold against my ass.

"You're not going to get in trouble from the principal, are you, Al?" I teased as I touched my clit and lowered my cunt toward her.

But she was sure of herself, and not thrown off. Before I expected it, she thrust so hard that the dong filled my cunt completely. I groaned and started speeding up my fingers on my clit. She kept thrusting and grunting while I reamed down on her, my clit swelling with each circle of my finger and each movement of her hips. I thought we might topple the porta-potty with our fucking. We kept on like that for five minutes at least. I clutched the wall behind her head when I came, dizzy with heat and the high, sweating even more than I had thought possible.

As I relaxed, I slid down her body and knelt between her legs. She spread them for me and I couldn't help but put my lips around the tip of her cock.

"Do it," she said. I looked up at her and she slowly moved the dong farther into my mouth. With one hand I shimmied the shaft and, while she watched, sucked her off to the taste of my own cunt juice.

Eventually, I leaned back and said, "So, you like to fuck, but do you like to *get* fucked?"

She raised her eyebrows in surprise. Then a grin, which she tried very hard to resist, curled at the corners of her mouth. Her tough-guy attitude was weakening. She glanced around the four square feet of porta-potty as though looking for an escape. Trying to keep her cockiness in check.

"Don't tell me you're late for math class," I said. At that she smiled full, grabbed my shirt, and started kissing me again.

"I'll take that as a yes."

I pushed her hard against the back wall and slid my hands down to find the buckle for her strap-on. Luckily they were only snaps. I unsnapped and shifted the cock out of the way of her cunt. We stopped kissing just so she could slide her ass toward the edge of the seat and give me easy access. I started playing with her clit and what a moan came from her. I shoved two fingers inside her and she started saying *please* between kisses. My other hand reached down so I could put another finger in her asshole. I began to thrust—thumb on her clit, two fingers in her cunt, and one in her ass. She grabbed around my ass and shirt to pull my body, thigh, arm, tight against her pussy while I fucked her. Her feet kicked at my hard hat on the floor and my hammer banged against her thigh as she came.

I cupped her cunt, and when she started to relax, just for the hell of it I slid my hand past her clit one more time, as far as I could get into her, only to have her come again, stifling long moans in my ear that told me this orgasm was twice as good as the last.

When Al eased her grip, I stood up and put my hand on the top of my hammer to stop it swinging on its hook.

She sat up on the john and turned her baseball hat around again.

"Nice hammer, Joe," she said.

"Estwing, twenty-one ounces." It was a good-sized hammer, I admit.

At that, we both struggled to put our pants back on, bumping asses as we did.

"Well, it was nice meeting ya, Al," I said, putting my hard hat back on my head.

We stood, staring at each other for a minute.

"Yah, well..." she said, gesturing to the outside, "...math class." She squeezed past me and out the door.

I laughed as it swung closed. Before leaving the box myself I took a few deep breaths and a long piss, relishing the thrill of getting to fuck her butch ass against a wall.

When I got back to the crew I heard an earful.

"Jesus, Joanne, where the hell have you been? We're gonna have this fucking house built without you."

"I had to piss like a race horse," I told them. Which was almost the truth.

Getting back to work, I fondled my hammer and wondered if anyone had noticed the porta-potty swaying a little in the invisible breeze of the day.

The Power of Language
S. Bear Bergman

Everyone has a type, right? No shame in that. Some people like zaftig brunettes, or gray flat-topped butches, or tall with green eyes, or short with a big ass, or any other combination of things. People laugh at me for the wide variety of my partners and say I'm a slut and I'll sleep with anyone, or they think I'm super broadminded, having shed in an oh-so-politically-correct manner any interest in something so superficial as a "type."

Neither one is really true, of course. I just go along, I never let on, but secretly I *do* have a type: writers.

What can I tell you? Bar none, writers are the best sex in the world. You want to really have a good time? Find a writer—preferably the kind who has at least dabbled in a little off-duty smut under an assumed name, and set about seducing her.

Start with some hot email. A little double entendre, a little innuendo, something about her filling up your in-box. Move from there. Let something slip, accidentally on purpose, that gives her some clues to your proclivities, and when she seizes on it like a hawk on a mouse, pretend to be shy. But don't be.

Be bolder, while playing at shyness; say, "I don't know what I was thinking, I usually don't talk about my sex life like that. I might mention that I was at the sex toy store, but *never* that while I was there I bought a nine-inch red and black latex dick, thinking of you using it on me, thinking about how good it would look in my mouth, about how that fat mushroom head would feel, rocking back and forth in my cunt, before you slid it all the way in, or anything like that."

The usual correspondent will reply and say, "Wow. That's so hot." And that's all very well and good. Nice to be appreciated. But a writer will go there with you, will see your bet and raise you, will reply: "Well. I certainly won't tell anyone about it, if that's what you're worried about, because I can understand how you might not want just *anyone* to know how hot you are for it, for me, how you can't wait to get down on your knees for me, take that fat cockhead in your mouth, how much you'll like it when I slide my dick in and out so slowly between your lips, one hand in your hair to keep you from getting more than I want you to have, how long I'll make you suck me before I'll let you have what you really want, before I'll pound into you and make you scream for me. I wouldn't want people to know things like that about me either, like that I love to get fucked up the ass, and that the image of your hands typing an email to me makes me think about each of those fingers in turn sliding into my tight ass, getting fucked sweet and slow with devilish precision until I start to whimper for more, please."

Now, you're in business. You've got her where you want her, right between your brain cells. You can keep talking about acts; there are lots of acts to discuss, trust me. You can confide how hot it makes you to have your nipples worked, petted and licked, twisted, chewed on, how it makes your cunt flood and your breath come fast and your hips pump, that it helps you get off, or that you love to make out and grope and squirm and hump with your hands under each other's shirts, working each other's tits, moaning into each other's mouths and clutching each other's necks, or how much you love the moment of getting your whole fist into a hot, wet cunt, when it just swallows you up, so trusting and so greedy, how the feel and sight of a hungry hole closing around your wrist makes you cream, that it floods you with a feeling so right, so intense, that you can't catch your breath and if you have something to hump against you can come just on that, without ever touching yourself.

Or, you can go a step further, and bring out the fantasies.

Everyone has them. No reason to be shy, who hasn't pretended to be something or someone, enacted some relationship or power dynamic, played the millionaire and the pool boy, the passenger and the flight attendant, two horny teenaged boys wrestling, the hitchhiker and the truck driver, the sailor and the whore, Brad and Jen, or some variation thereof? And if you haven't, I bet you've wanted to, haven't you? Thought to yourself some line of dialogue that only makes sense in the context of a fantasy, like "Hurry, my husband will be home any minute!" or "Get off me before I call the cops," or "Let's meet behind the Arts and Crafts Shack after lights out," or "For five hundred dollars, I could find some time." Whatever it is. Because writers? Writers are *great* with fantasies, writers will role-play with you flawlessly, it's in their nature to inhabit a character and flesh it out, so when you shyly confide, via a haltingly written email that takes two hours to compose, that you want to play teenagers on a study date who get going on the sofa and that you want to be the good girl who gets talked out of her virginity by the senior boy, you'll start getting email in character from the writer, currently corresponding as "Steve," who will write things like:

Hey—My folks are going to be out that night at a charity dinner in the city. So if you still want to come over and watch

*a movie that's cool, but you probably better tell your folks
you're at Vanessa's house because they probably won't be
too cool with you being all alone with me at my house unless
they're way cooler than my parents. What do you want to
watch? Steve.*

And when you arrive she will be all excited to have stolen
two nip bottles of Jack Daniels from a friend's house, and will
insist on pouring one into your Diet Coke, and will have actually rented a movie and dimmed the living room lights and
will put the movie on and wait twenty, maybe thirty minutes
before getting up and going into the kitchen and coming back
and sitting right down next to you, and will as authentically
as possible tentatively put a hand on your chest and then
under your shirt until the action gets so hot that she starts
using all her skills and only the talking is still Steve, "Yeah,
baby, aw, just kiss it, it'll make me feel so good, c'mon, look
how hard it is for you, don't be a tease, honey, you know you
want to," and you'll be so wet, and so hot for it, but you'll
say, "I dunno, Stevie, I never did that before," and it'll be so
good like that, pushing and pulling, teasing and cajoling and
hesitating and starting again, all night, until you're bent over
the back of the sofa with your jeans around your ankles getting fucked hard, just like you like it, and she's saying, "I sure
am glad you came over to watch a movie, babe."

That's what writers are good for.

Or you'll mention that you always wanted to pick someone up at a bar and take them out to your car and do them
in the backseat, and she'll write back, and name a time, and
a place, and when you arrive there she'll be, decked out in a
crisp shirt and leather pants, and you'll start talking—buy her
a drink, buy her another one, start sliding one hand up her
thigh until she's sitting on the barstool with her knees apart
and you're standing between her legs, the dildo that you're
packing making a long bulge in your jeans, rubbing it against

her, rocking it into her crotch when some hip-hop comes on the juke box, and before long you're chewing on her earlobe and breathing in her ear, murmuring, "God, I can't wait to fuck you," until she picks her head up and says, "Let's go," and you get out to the parking lot, to your little Ford, and unlock the door for her and she reaches around and unlocks the door to the backseat and says, "Let's get in here, for a minute," and you grin, and agree, and pretty soon she's on your lap, your cock deep in her cunt, and she's bouncing up and down on your tool while you work her nipples with your teeth and pull her hard against your dick, and she gasps, "I never, I've never...I can't believe I'm...holy shit, yes, right there, just like that, so good," and you'll grin like a wolf in the dim sodium lamplight and say, "That's right, so hot, you don't know anything about me, do you, and you don't care, you just need a hard cock, just need to get fucked, that's right, fuck yourself on my cock..." until she comes, shuddering, all over your lap, and collapses into your arms, and you grin in the hot car, and think about how glad you are that you know enough to proposition writers, and what you might like to play next week.

Morality Tail
Fiona Zedde

Kai groaned with frustration. Buried deep in the business section of the newspaper was yet another article about an independent bookstore closing its doors. Her own bookstore, Brownstone, had been recording steadily declining sales for the past four years. Still, she managed to hold on. A few weeks ago she had read in that same business section about a chain bookstore that in less than two years would open its doors only a mile from Brownstone. Although she was an optimist by nature, every day was a struggle not to worry about what she would do when those two years were up.

Kai looked up from her newspaper when a flash of color caught her eye. She knew that red hair. It belonged to Mandla Richards, a neighborhood dyke and a welcome distraction from her grim thoughts. She watched as the tall woman sailed through the parking lot. Her fox-red kinky curls bounced around a face that was nothing less than gorgeous—full, pouty mouth; dimpled cheeks; and heavy-lidded eyes that led inevitably to thoughts of fucking. A dress the color of iced coffee—the same tempting shade as her skin—hugged her full shape.

Mandla was the girl whom Vivian, Kai's most recent and painful ex, had left her for. Even after all this time Kai couldn't understand what the attraction was, although she did spend many sweat-soaked nights imagining the women doing all kinds of things together, their heaving, heavy breasts, their mouths open to explore every inch of available flesh.

Mandla now was walking into the large chain bookstore next door to the natural foods market where Kai sat having a solitary late dinner and reading the paper. *What the hell was she doing over there? She'd better not be shopping.* Soon Kai finished, stood up, and left, to pack away her groceries in her Honda convertible. The car's alarm chirped as she locked it and walked toward the bookstore.

Chain store robots perked up enough to look up as she walked through the door: a tall, slim woman with her thick hair shaped in a high, perfectly round Afro around a face of interesting angles and lines. She was handsome in her black slacks, tank top, and the open long-sleeved shirt that accentuated the lean grace of her body. Kai's nipples instantly hardened in the too-cold store. She hissed in annoyance. Her eyes searched for the fire-haired woman.

She found Mandla in the philosophy section, standing in front of an overcrowded bookshelf with her head bent over a thick hardcover book. Her back was turned to Kai in the narrow dead-end aisle, allowing the slim woman ample time to appreciate her elegant back, the rounded ass, the long bare legs under the dress.

"Mandla." Kai greeted the woman with a smile that was not.

The other woman looked up, then colored faintly with embarrassment at being caught in this particular bookstore. "Oh, hello. Kai, right?"

Of course she knew who Kai was. The dyke rumor mill had buzzed with news of how badly Kai had treated Vivian. More than likely dwelling on details of her love of silk scarves and leather straps. All the better to please you with, my dear, Kai had always told Vivian. Back then, her ex-girlfriend had sighed in wicked delight when Kai had contorted her incredibly limber body into pleasure-inducing positions on the four-poster bed. And had teased and fucked her until she dripped wet with satisfaction. *That* was treating her badly? As far as Kai saw it, she just hadn't treated Vivian like the princess that she thought she was. And Kai was willing to bet that this was also the reason Mandla had become another ex.

"Yes, I'm Kai. You met me at the Wine's Chalice a few months ago." She named a local antique shop owned by mutual friends, a dyke couple who'd relocated fifteen years ago from Miami, Kai's hometown. "When you and Viv were still together."

Kai remembered the meeting very well, recalled the tight pants that had hugged Mandla's high, phat ass like a jealous lover, the back-baring halter top that had begged for Kai's teeth to loosen its string then follow the path that the smooth valley of her spine had led to.... Yeah, she remembered the meeting, remembered thinking that it was going to be hard seeing Vivian with her new girl, but had instead gotten a fierce clit hard-on that led her around the party sniffing after her ex's current, longing to ride that thick, firm ass to glory. Mandla hadn't been oblivious to her need either. The fire-haired woman had looked too long into her eyes once, seen the burn of desire, and, Kai thought, flickered alight with a companion flame.

"Ah." Mandla's eyes flickered over Kai now, lingering a moment too long on the stiffened nipples still visible through the two layers of cloth.

Kai smiled, wondering exactly what Vivian had told

Mandla about her. Then she made herself comfortable on the low bench in the middle of the aisle. "So, what brings you to this place?"

Mandla looked around as if it should be obvious to Kai what she was doing in a bookstore. But her polite southern upbringing couldn't let her say the words out loud.

"I'm looking for a Cixous book with a particular essay in it."

"Brownstone on the Square has a pretty nice selection of books by French feminists. Did you go there first?"

"No, I didn't think they would have what I needed." Mandla shrugged and managed to look uncomfortable and sexy at the same time. "Besides, it's an inconvenient drive."

Kai watched as the other woman's cleavage rearranged itself in her neckline. The peaks of Mandla's breasts winked at her. *Guess she's cold too*, she thought with a wry grin.

"Honey, you only live a mile or two from the square. How is that an inconvenient drive?"

Mandla's polite smile disappeared. "Are you stalking me? Why do you know where I live, and what do you want?" she said with a sharp tone.

"Calm down. I'm not stalking anyone. I just wanted to say hi to you and remind you about supporting independent bookstores. They all need the support right now, especially with stores like this one," she said, waving a hand to encompass the cool, sterile place where they talked, "actively trying to put them out of business."

"What are you, an ad for the small business co-op? I'll spend my money wherever I choose."

"How about spending your money to support a community that supports you? When you want that lesbian romance novel, it's the independent store that you come to. Why don't you buy your other books there too?"

"You're not going to bully me into something I don't want

to do." *Just like you bullied Vivian.* The unsaid phrase hung in the air between them.

Kai stood up. "I didn't bully Vivian. What I did do was allow her to be free of her own mental restrictions for a while. She gave herself to me. I didn't have to force anything from her."

Mandla flushed, from the sweet swell of her breasts to her fiery hairline. The book in her hands fluttered closed.

"Would you like to know how it feels?" Kai glanced around quickly to make sure their aisle was empty.

Mandla put her book away. "I didn't come here to be harassed by you."

But Kai caught the flare of interest in her eyes. She wasn't the only one with an itch. "Then why did you come here?" She stepped closer to the other woman.

"Vivian was definitely right about you." Mandla put a hand against Kai's chest to ward her off.

"What did she say about me?"

"That you were a bully, of course."

"Hmm." Her voice rumbled deep in her throat as the hand on her chest began to move in slow circles. "What else?"

"That you liked power games."

"Yes. And?"

"That you were an awful girlfriend."

Kai laughed. "Well, you know what I said about the bullying."

"Hm-hmm. That she wanted it."

"As for the other things she said, why don't you try me out and see?"

It was Mandla's turn to laugh. "Pretty sure of yourself, aren't you?"

"And getting surer by the second." Kai swallowed. "May I touch you?"

"What?"

"You heard me."

Mandla's eyes flickered around the deserted aisle. "What are you going to do?"

"Answer my question first." Kai licked her lips, watching the quickening rise and fall of Mandla's firm breasts. A fine coat of sweat covered them despite the artificially cold air.

"Sure. Why not?"

Kai laughed again and stepped even closer until Mandla's back was against the bookshelves. "Was that a yes?"

The full-hipped woman cleared her throat and blushed again. "Yes."

"Turn around."

The two women were the same height and fit easily together: Mandla's ass in the bed of Kai's hips, the curve of the other woman's back against Kai's belly.

"If I do anything you don't want, feel free to call on one of the helpful sales associates. I'm sure they'd be more than happy to come to your aid." Kai's hand slid up Mandla's thigh, moving the dress out of her way. She bit the other woman's ear, licked the soft skin at the back of her neck. Kai braced her booted foot on the bottom shelf of the bookcase. Her shirt flapped open like wings to hide Mandla's thighs and the movement of her hand between them. She pressed her face in Mandla's hair, inhaling its faint scent of coconuts.

A low groan left her throat when she realized that Mandla had left her panties at home. Kai's fingers found her wet, already swollen with need for her touch. Mandla released her breath in a slow hiss and dropped her head back onto Kai's shoulder. Her thumb brushed Mandla's swollen clit, drawing another hiss from the woman.

"Inside," she murmured against Kai's ear. "Please." Kai slid her fingers into the waiting wet pussy. Her ass rotated against Kai, pushing back into the seam of her slacks and bumping the already sensitive clit. She widened her legs and pushed against Mandla's ass. They both groaned.

"Faster, please."

Her shoulder straps slid down and her breasts fell free, revealing fat juicy nipples that begged to be sucked and swallowed by Kai's hungry mouth. Kai worked her mouth on the other woman's neck instead, biting the soft flesh that strained and vibrated under her touch. Mandla bit her lip but she still panted, making loud, urgent sounds that moved Kai's hips faster against her, in rhythm with the slick pussy riding her pistoning fingers and the thumb vibrating against her clit. Mandla's soft cries increased in volume, becoming urgent pants and moans that, in another place, Kai would have been glad to hear. Although the angle was awkward, Kai kissed her and swallowed the noise. She cupped a breast in her hand, pinched the responsive nipples as her hand slid between Mandla's soft thighs, working the slick pussy that was beginning to clench around her fingers.

Mandla's knee jerked against the shelf, knocking books loose. They dropped to the floor with a soft thud like footsteps, like the sound of urgency. Mandla spasmed, gushed, and came, shouting into her mouth, fingers clenched around the edge of the bookshelf. With a soft whimper, she pushed Kai's hand away. But the other woman wasn't finished yet.

"Wait," she rasped, grabbing Mandla's clothed hips. "Don't move."

Her sensitive nipples felt hot and tight inside her shirt. She rubbed them against Mandla's back. Fire pulled tight in her belly, burning her from the inside out and peppering her body with sweat. She sighed when Mandla dropped her head forward and pushed back, grinding her ass into Kai's pussy, bringing her closer to the relief she needed. She grabbed the soft hips tighter and thrust against that firm, luscious ass until the electric flickers of sensation darting between her nipples and her clit overwhelmed her. Kai gave up her control as she came, shuddering against Mandla's ass and panting into her neck.

"Thank you," Kai said, bracing herself against the bookshelf before stepping slowly back. Mandla rearranged her dress and turned to face her.

"No. Thank *you*." She licked her lips and wiped at the moisture gathered above them. Her breath still came in ragged little gasps.

They both stepped away to lean against opposite bookshelves and admire the freshly fucked look the other wore.

"Don't you own a bookstore?" Mandla asked, when she could speak again.

"Yes." Kai nodded. "The one on the Square."

"So let me guess, you want me to come there instead of here?"

"Ideally, yes." Kai reached into her wallet for a business card, then scribbled her cell number on it. "But in case you want it somewhere more comfortable, give me a call. I'm sure we can arrange something."

Mandla slid the card between her damp breasts. "I'll do that." She picked up her purse from where it had fallen on the floor. "See you around."

With a twitch of her behind, she turned and walked out of the bookstore. Empty handed.

Of Goddesses and Expletives
Lynne Jamneck

Ow—fuck!

That's how it started. And with that, pretty much, I should have known it wouldn't be your run-of-the-mill fling. Or affair. Situation. Whatever. Besides, I didn't really believe in affairs. I prefer to allude to them as encounters. Of the hot kind, sexy kind, upside-down kind (yes…), outrageous kind—although that basically sums up the upside-down bit, and then some.

A girl has to build her repertoire.

Anyway. Closer to the point.

The only thing I had been intent on building that couple of contractual days had been the six-foot statue of Athena that the Women's League of Cape Town had commissioned for their annual meeting of angry minds.

SLAM: Women Without Borders Against the World.

Or something to that effect.

I'd rolled my eyes the first time I had heard it, and a couple of times after that, too. Sometimes I get the feeling that women were their own worst enemies. Half of the white noise we are always battling against is our own.

But—I digress. It's a flaw. It might happen again. Just a warning. But sometimes it happens in exactly the right place, so it might be worth sticking around, if you catch my drift.

The money was good and I had no problems spending a couple of days carving plaster of paris, even though I did think it a bit ludicrous that it should be Athena—a *patriarchal* god—instead of, say, Mother Africa or Gaia. Or is that the same thing? My mythology isn't nearly up to scratch.

So there I was, chipping away at the left boob of a woman who had supposedly sprung from the forehead of her lightning-obsessed father, fully grown and ready for battle.

Granted, such a birth would piss many a lass off, and there were more than a couple of those milling about in the Civic Center where the big bash would be taking place over three feminist-fueled days the following week. Maybe Athena had been a prudent choice after all.

"You'd better make sure both of those are the same size."

On all accounts, it was the voice that made me look up from Athena's developing 34C cups, and not the comment.

She didn't appear typical of every other woman I'd noticed hanging around. Layered, red hair. Wispy. Un-elf-like, thank god. Generous mouth, but not too Julia Robertsy. Tilted upward in a curious, encouraging smile. Femininely touched combat pants, topped by a sexy, spaghetti-strapped vest. I wondered if she would be offended if I asked her to strip. She'd be the perfect mirror to my goddess construction.

"What will they do if they're not? The same size, I mean?" I kept chipping away, losing focus fast. "Accuse me of discrimination?"

She laughed, quietly. It was enough of a distraction for me to catch both myself and the chisel off-guard. The hammer hit my thumb, dead center.

"Ow—fuck!"

People turned to look, irate at the vulgarity, but the red-headed Athena blocked their view and took my bruised, plaster-powdered finger between her hands. Warm, the inside of her palm, fingers slender, curling around mine. I noticed cool, blue veins rising below the skin of her hands. Tried not to say "Ow" again as the blood rushed in my ears and my thumb kept aching. Athena kissed my bruised thumb. How quickly this commission had turned into something quite unanticipated.

"That must happen to your fingers all the time," she said, looking at me in a concerned fashion that did not completely belie her intentions. Plaster powder decorated her cheek where she had held my hand. I resisted the urge to reach out and brush it off. I kind of liked the look of my mark on her. I felt as if I was the director of my own private movie.

"Sometimes," I answered uncertainly, and admittedly a bit unsteadily. I recognized the due process of swooning, its onset in this particular scenario coming on in quick, rapid measures. Usually this would be an infliction *I* induce. I'm a pretty damned good little charmer. But there was a certain personal weakness at work here that was playing havoc with my regular seduction process.

The Older Woman.

She couldn't have been more than thirty-six, maybe thirty-seven at the very most. I was a healthy, horny, and strapping twenty-eight, ready to give in to my Achilles heel.

Shoes, slinky lingerie, whips, leather, ropes.... People adhere to the rules of their attractions in myriad ways. Most of the time they don't even recognize where these naughty preferences originated from in their potent, primal subconscious. I had a girlfriend once who liked nothing more than to be fucked at the left corner of an intersection, ten minutes after sunset. Any other time of the day, no intersection, the wrong side of the road—forget it. No action. But get the small details of her sexual incentive correct, and you could get her to do anything. Like the time I gave her an intersection in exchange for a particularly well-executed fuck in the board-room of Davidtz & Son, the law firm where she had made partner just before we met. It had been one of those Fantastic Fucks. Not that hard to come by, but a glorious little blessing to one's everyday everyday, you know? I gave it to her on the enormous, polished oak table, portraits of her male colleagues looking on in frozen, jealous, stunned silence. I wasn't fuck-ing stupid. I knew very well how every single one of them had wanted to do the same.

See? Again, I get distracted.

Older women. Right.

They're very particular about what they want, and how they want it.

"Why Athena?" Red wanted to know.

"Not too sure myself," I answered vaguely. The dim throb in my thumb competed for the not so dim hammer of lust coursing through my blood.

"Look, you're going to have to tell me your name. I keep referring to you in my head as 'Red.'"

She smiled coyly. "You don't even know my name and already you're thinking about me."

The hammer felt heavy in my hand. I was vaguely aware of the steady hum of voices talking in drone-dialect, filling the outside world, the rest of space that wasn't me and—

"Emily."

Emily. Such a pretty, innocent name for someone with buckets of sex appeal. I realized that I must have looked fairly hilarious standing there, chisel in one hand, hammer in the other, and the obvious calamity my body found itself in writ-ten all over my face. Powered and immobilized by excitement at the same time. Expectation. It had something to do with that anecdote about intersections I'd rambled on about earlier.

The people whom I knew were looking at us.

Athena, towering half-carved behind me.

And in real life, Emily standing in front of me, one hand on her exquisitely fashioned boyish hip, waiting for me to explore the other hidden details of her meant-for-sex form.

It was movie time.

I placed my tools by the feet of the unfinished goddess and took Emily's hand.

She came willingly.

This is always a good sign.

Bless me, the bathrooms were down the first, nearest corridor. Shiny green and white tiling, lots of polished mirrors. I felt like a dirty Alice in Wonderland.

Emily pulled me into the nearest open stall. These things always appear bigger than they actually are. It was cramped, and then some. Every Roger Ramjet and his aunty knew that people screwed in public toilets. A law should be introduced to make them even smaller.

He-he.

Nothing like having to struggle for what you want.

With one hand still working the insubordinate latch on the pristine-white stall door, Emily turned and kissed me.

It was hot—if ever such a description could be satisfactory. Her hand, now finished with the door, was working its way up past the edge of my dirty T-shirt.

"Fuck—"

"Shhh," I replied.

"What?"

"Quiet...I don't want to get caught."

"I didn't say anything." Her hands unbuttoning my bra, Emily kissed me again. Positively stuck her delicious tongue down my throat. My own hands were cupping the firm roundness of her butt, rubbing and feeling the smooth skin beneath her practical cotton panties. The stall became warm despite the air conditioning.

"Oh, fuck—"

We both stopped. Looked at one another. I held a trembling finger to my lips.

The stall next to us. Shuffling feet.

"Oh."

"Like this?"

"Yes, oh yes—just like that."

"Don't—fuck, oh fuck, yes…"

Emily's eyes gleamed mischievously. Her mouth was inches from mine. Maybe she wasn't Athena after all. Or maybe she had swallowed Loki when I hadn't been looking. Regardless—I had a live one here. The two disembodied voices next door didn't seem to be aware of us. Alternatively, maybe they just didn't care. Emily mouthed an authoritatively instructed *keep quiet*—more because it was what she wanted at that point than out of any sense of embarrassment, I gathered. She pushed me away, leaned back against the stall-divide, and peeled off the feeble excuse for a top she was wearing. And lo—she wasn't wearing a bra. I didn't need any further encouragement.

Her nipples were hard even before my lips touched them, Emily's hands fisting in my hair as I took each nipple in turn between my teeth.

Heavy breathing from next door. Something falling on the floor followed by a clinking sound. Belt buckle, possibly. It was a righteous fucking effort to keep quiet. Emily used both hands on my hips to pull me closer, a leg for good measure snaking around tight against my hip. Slowly we fell into one another, her naked skin warm through the weathered fabric of my shirt, her hard nipples against my ribs. Our tongues behaved languidly, and it was slow and hot again, an unexpected mix of sexy, needy, and familiar. My hand explored permissively down the inside of her thigh, getting more insistent as Emily's tongue became more demanding inside my mouth. She directed me onto the sturdy, butch silver buttons of her cargo pants, her leg slipping between mine, pulling us as close as we could possibly get. Her heat radiated, reached out to me.

The buttons undone, my hand past the sensible boundaries of her underwear, ripping it aside, thrusting inside her and—oh my fucking god—how extremely tight and wet she was. I looked down, past the folds of tightly stretched clothing, clinging like second skins, and saw that she had some tribal design tattoo that ran down from her navel and disappeared into the front of her panties. It moved like a snake, undulating as she worked against my hand.

A body next door thudded twice against the divider.

A throaty, suppressed laughed escaped Emily's lips.

I began fucking her as quietly as possible under the circumstances, my head spinning, eyes swimming. She experimented with a variety of tactics to keep silent: pulled on my hair (which almost made *me* give us away), tugging at my shirt (which I could feel was chafing my skin). Threw her head back against the stall wall, throat exposed, bit down on her lips, top and bottom. Looked into the darkly lit pools of my black eyes, lips slightly parted, eyelids fluttering. I concentrated on the coolness of the wall against the back of my hand as I gripped her ass, pulling her onto me. Helping the rhythm of her intent, charging down the road closer to her own intersection, fucking closer, and then she did make a noise—at least, the back of her head banged against the cubicle. Twice. Remarkably, she was quiet, at least in words or sounds, as the inspiring, tight cord of an orgasm ripped through her.

"Ow—fuck!" a woman's voice yelled in ecstasy from next door.

Third time's a charm.

We waited. Clinging to one another. Everything was quiet. Neither of us dared breathe too loudly. Eventually we heard a door open. Two quiet sets of footfalls hurriedly left the rest-room.

"Did you know," Emily eventually whispered in my ear, "that Athena shunned the sexual advances of her fellow gods?"

I bent down and kissed the soft, downy hair running down her stomach, the snake tattoo.

"I know. She loved mortals too much."

Surrounded, Surrender
Barbara Brown

It's a sleepy night. The mist has rolled in off the ocean and surrounded us, enveloping our small home on this island, creating a dark and safe place. It feels like living in a cave, if caves were made of pillows. Sitting on the porch with the misty chill pushing against my skin, I rest my head against the billowy cave walls. Their suppleness holds no grudge against my shifting movements, just like my mother's womb. I love being embraced by the softness of the sky. I could step off my porch and walk through it without effort. The mist will part for me and will still surround me, its presence seemingly endless. The wet air sends a tingling down my back and pleasure into my heart. I sink further into my chair, into myself, with absolute content. I am exactly where I want to be, although I couldn't always have said that.

When we first moved here I used to fight with the clouds. Ruann didn't understand. To her, they were innocuous creatures floating through our lives. They were there or they weren't and she'd just shake her sexy butt out into them, going wherever she was going. I'd watch her, tiny and tough, striding into the fog. It gave her pleasure. Me, I loved the brazenness of harvest-time farmland stretching into deep blue nothingness. The clouds' softness irritated me. I wanted something more from them if they were going to be so close. I wanted something firmer than the clouds could ever be.

My fighting was useless. The clouds always won. Just like my ex. He had no substance, at least not that I could feel. I would hit out and pass through what was supposed to be him. I'd try and wrestle but it was like Jacob fighting with the wind. I couldn't grab hold of anything. There was no resistance and it drove me crazy. It drove me to leave the relationship. When I found someone who was as strong as I was, who would fight tooth and nail to keep herself, I knew I'd come home. Her strength woke me up, turned me on. I found my equal in Ruann, and we loved and fought hard to prove it.

"How dare you decide to go home for Christmas without even talking to me about it?"

"Ruann, it's family tradition—we all come home. Always. It's not a choice."

"It is."

"My parents aren't used to the idea of us yet. It's hasn't been that long since I told them."

"It's almost a year. You just don't want to be uncomfortable."

"Eight months. Whether you're there or not, Christmas with my parents will be anything but comfortable, and you know it. So don't guilt me into this. Besides, you've repeatedly said you can't stand the prairies, let alone in winter. And, you're Jewish. Why the big deal about Christmas?"

"That's not the point. Your parents have to deal with us. Your brother's bringing his wife and Josie's bringing her boyfriend. You didn't even ask me."

"Kevin's going to be there."

"What?"

"Kevin's going to..."

"I heard you, I just can't believe it. You invited your ex?"

"My parents did."

"Fuck them. And fuck you. Have a merry Christmas."

The worst of our verbal battles took us well into the night. Both unwilling to end the struggle, we fought in a way that reduced us to flinging nastiness across the growing chasm. Finally, exhausted and emptied, we crashed on opposite sides of the room. We gave way to sleep but didn't leave our posts. We had not reached resolution. Either of us could have left during that time—hoisted ourselves up and crawled out the door—but neither of us did.

I was woken by the reflection of the half-moon peering over the building across the street. Its beam illuminated Ruann sprawled across the hardwood floor with a corner of flannel blanket pulled over her still dressed, wiry body. Her face was ragged and her clenched fist clung to the fleecy cover as she lay there, on the same floor as me, as sore and alone and exhausted as I was. Her salt and pepper hair made her look old in that light. I crawled to her side of the room, lay down beside her, and passed out. When I woke up she was holding my hand. That's how I realized for the first time in thirty-seven years that I didn't have to be alone.

In the ten years since, we moved and set up home in this artists' community landscaped by beaches, old-growth forest, and wet. Our blue board house has one bedroom, kitchen, living room, and too much stuff from Montreal.

Within the first year, Ruann's brother asked to live with us. I absolutely refused. I wasn't going to let my threatened space be further invaded. She felt she had to say yes—no one else could host him and she was deeply missing family she left behind. The argument lasted weeks, riding the brink of ending. At last, we compromised. We found him a place to stay on the island with his days spent at our house. Ruann relaxed into hanging at home with Ari and me, and let go of tooling around with the island's rowdier lesbian crowd. I was surprised at the ease of our transition and how we managed to settle. Crammed so close together, we thought we'd rip each other to shreds, but we didn't. It was good. We ate well, did lots of laughing, and fixed up the place. Along with that compromise, Ruann and I agreed, "No more fighting." The relief was overwhelming and, mostly, the struggle didn't seem necessary any longer.

The change was so slow we hardly noticed. Ari returned east after a year and I stopped trying to win my fight with the clouds. The wet dampened both my spirits and my desire. It was a fight I couldn't win. Chilled, I wrapped myself in the blanket of our home and the love we had built, believing I was safe. The house shrank in around me. Ruann began going out more. I stopped being interested in sex. The blanket and her absence became walls in our limited space.

The settling was costly.

It is as hot as it ever gets here, which isn't very. I want to feel the sun on my skin the way a prairie sun feels in a blue summer sky, but clouds are crowding the sun out. Again. Humidity coats the air and makes me feel that old craziness when I can't fight with something. I have learned to quell this anxious feeling since coming here, although I don't know exactly where it has gone. There isn't room to put things away here.

Ruann comes up behind me as I tidy the small living space. Putting her hand on my shoulder she says, "Talk to me."

I continue, bending over to move a book on the table. I dust under the book and return it to its exact spot. Her hand slips off my shoulder.

"Talk to me," she says again with startling urgency. I walk

away. Entering our bedroom, I crumple on the bed, a silent scattering of fear and frustration and loneliness. There are no tears and no words. I don't know how to say how caught I feel, powerless, lost. The front door clicks closed. Her rusty Jeep door squeaks open, then closed. My ears are waiting for the effortful rumble of the old engine turning over, but it doesn't come. Instead, Ruann is walking into our bedroom with a flyer in her hand. Her green eyes are icy turquoise, like the outer harbor in winter.

Tossing the flimsy paper onto the bedspread beside me she says, "I'm going. "

I glance at it cursorily, this gaudy thing resting between us, then push past Ruann to take it out of the bedroom. I discard it on a stack of other community flyers that Ruann brings in from outside—brochures about what's going on in the art community, the dyke community, the political scene. She leaves them around the house. I collect them into a bundle and use them for fire starter. The first line on this one reads, "First time ever! The island's sexiest, hottest place to be... GottaGetSome."

A woman's bathhouse. Here, on the island. It's ridiculous. Who is going to do anything in this little place? How sexy can anyone be dressed in fleece and wool, or under a sky that crowds and suffocates? Who are we trying to be? I leave the flyer's bold print screaming at the old linoleum and salt-air-peeling paint, picking up my rag to finish the interrupted dusting. Its large letters play at the periphery of my vision wherever I go in this tiny box, irritating the calm I am trying to create. The unending haunting sends me out. I walk slowly to the bay that has become my sanctuary, the place where sometimes I can see a rolling field of wheat, an open sky. I look out as far as I can, over the ripples of shore waves, the chaos of eddies where the water deepens, the long slow undulations of ocean. There is no horizon today, lost in a blur of air-suspended water. I fill my lungs with screams that can't blow the fog away.

Hours later when I return, she has gone to bed. The flyer is where I left it and so is my dust rag. I want both to be out of my sight. I sit at the kitchen table and flick at the corner of the flyer, reading the whole thing. Apparently they are renting a hot tub from the mainland and putting it into the community hall. There will be a local jazz trio playing and a make-your-own lingerie contest. The bathhouse is Saturday night, two nights and three weeks away. My guess is Ruann's known about this for a while, but I'm not sure she planned to tell me. It's not that we haven't gone to these things before. We have—in Montreal, New York—in our early years. Our fighting years. But we left all that behind. We're passed that. How can she say she's going? I leave the dog-eared brochure on the table with the others, certain I will not be there with her.

That Saturday arrives and Ruann spends the day fussing over her wardrobe and pulling out her toys. She's chatty, wondering aloud who of this insular community is brave enough to go.

"What if I'm the only one?" she asks without expectation of an answer. Each time she opens her mouth to speak, I brace myself for the attack. For the demand. Perhaps she is waiting for me to beg her to stay home. None of these happen. We eat dinner in silence. She doesn't touch her food. I wolf mine down.

When she gets up from the table, she asks, "Are you coming with me?"

"No," I reply and see a small tear gather in her eye, which she doesn't bother to wipe away.

"Okay, goodnight then," and she leaves, revving the engine for a while before driving off.

After the growling of the truck fades, the house is quiet. I imagine what I might do with my night—play the music I love and Ruann does not, eat ice cream until I feel sick but love it anyway, write, work on my latest glass piece…but two hours later I am still sitting by the window, totally aware of the flyer on the table stained from dinner's spaghetti sauce. It is at least a half-hour drive to the community center. I could easily miss her. She's probably on her way home right now. I start rummaging through the junk we couldn't part with when we left Montreal. There are still boxes full of papers, mementos, knick-knacks. I'm tired of them. High school yearbooks, stay. Glass unicorn figurine, goes. Journals, burn.

The fire is crackling with yesterday's words when a large drawing falls from an old coil binder. It's from a class where we danced from the different systems of our bodies—bones, joints, muscles, fluids, and internal organs—then drew our experience. Hardly a picture, only gigantic, bloody letters declaring, "I can't go there! I hate it." It was my organs. Others in the group, I remember, had soft, round images of warm oranges, reds, and yellows. They talked about feeling comfort. The fire has petered out but I throw the picture on it anyway and watch it slowly char. Another hour ticks by.

My brain is spinning faster than my feet can travel. I am pacing the ten steps from front door to living room, the full length of our house. I have lost track of the number of times I've covered this ground. How dare she go? What is she doing? It's people we know and she's there on her own, cruising island dykes. What are they going to think? It's okay. Nothing will happen and she'll be home soon. The whole thing is totally silly. They're probably sitting around talking about their gardens. But, what if she picks someone up? Or someone picks her up? Or she has sex with everyone? Humiliation washes over me, then anger, then humiliation again, then fear. I grab my bag and key and get into the one extravagance we afford ourselves—the second vehicle. The flyer becomes a crumpled mess in my hand.

With the rows of Jeeps, 4x4s, and a few VW cars parked

outside, the community center-turned-bathhouse is unmistakable. It could be a dyke convention or, minus the VWs,
the parking lot of a prairie tavern. I wish it were the latter.
I would know how to hold myself if I needed to walk into a
tavern. The number of cars corralled around the hall is enough
to know the answer to Ruann's earlier question. My churning
stomach drops out from under me, and my breath along with
it. I will have to face this. Her. I park at the end of a long row
and tentatively walk toward the entrance.

Motion-sensor spotlights announce my arrival to no one.
The deflating balloons they light are anything but welcoming. Or sexy. I expect the same inside, gaudy, tacky, childish,
but when I enter, the atmosphere is quiet and heated. It feels
like a kettle before it boils, waiting and wanting to erupt. A
woman, easily in her late fifties, dressed in short-shorts and
an elastic tube top, hands me a large plastic bag for storage.
She looks good, a glow of pleasure about her. She's having
fun. I return her smile and she air-kisses me, European-style.
My cheeks burn with embarrassment. Embarrassment that
her generosity has moved me, and that I don't know her. She
feels like she belongs here.

I scan the room, what little I can see of it, but don't spot
Ruann. Drapes of heavy fabric—plush, fake velvet—line the
walls and create a maze of the space. Steam from the hot
tub is drifting over one drape. The overdone sensuality of it,
sweetly sexy and friendly, pulls me in and reminds me of why
we moved here.

Our friends, Ginny and Rita, described the island as "a
place of quiet bliss, a lane of content neighbors who look
damn good in saggy pants and flop-brimmed hats." What
looked good when we visited was the feel of the place. We
saw only the ideal. When we visited, it was sunny. It was a
thrill to decide to move here.

The long-ago excitement mixes with the drifting heat and

smell of women's bodies, sending a twinge of energy through my own. I can be here for me. I square my shoulders, find my stride, and walk into the charged space. Stripping down to my jockeys and undershirt, I throw my stuff in the bag provided by the mystery woman at the front door and sit resting against a plush-lined wall near the rented hot tub. There are cushions thrown around the floor and exercise mats with blankets. A woman with long blonde hair and tight little breasts walks by me and "accidentally" brushes up against my leg. My leg feels like it's shimmering where she touched.

"Excuse me," she murmurs. I motion for her to sit down with lackadaisical Montreal savvy. This is how I like to be.

"I don't think we've met before," she stutters. "I'm Jessica. I just moved to the island a month ago. It seemed like such a nice place. The first time I saw it I wanted to live here, but I didn't have the money to buy land and couldn't figure out how I'd manage, but then I heard about the organic farm that Shan and Ted are running. So I'm living with them and helping with the farm. You know, I've never been to anything like this before, so I'm not really sure what I want to do. So I hope you won't think that I'm just here for sex, 'cause that's not it. That's not it at all. I was kind of curious. I've never, *ever* done anything like this before. I grew up in Vancouver, but I never really liked it there, and I don't think this kind of thing happens there. I don't know. I never found out. You know, I've never even slept with a woman, although I think I might like to. But I'm not sure. I don't even really know what to do."

She pauses. She made it through her monologue without passing out. I am impressed by her feat but becoming less interested.

"Oh, I'm sorry. I must seem like an idiot, and you probably aren't even attracted to me and I don't need to worry about setting all those boundaries, and things. You aren't, are you?" she asks with hope and trepidation.

She finally pauses to breathe. "You're a beautiful woman," she says with a smile, dropping her eyes—a female habit I dislike greatly—"but I'm not sure I'm here for sex either. Maybe we make a good match."

"Oh. You're not here for sex?"

"No. Not with strangers."

And then I see Ruann coming out of one of the small rooms down the hall, meeting rooms converted for tonight's event. She doesn't look happy exactly, but she doesn't look unhappy. My heart sinks at the thought of what has happened in that room.

"Excuse me," I say to Jessica and get up to leave. Ruann sees me and her face ripples with emotions I don't know anymore. I drop my eyes as she approaches, look up coyly, mimicking Jessica's action. I touch her shoulder lightly and hate myself with every attempt to entice her this way.

"Hi," I say, smiling like a twelve-year-old girl who's never been kissed but desperately wants to be. "I was hoping we might, uh, well…" My voice falters. I run out of words.

"Don't do that," she says. "If you want me, tell me or show me, but don't play with me. You wouldn't talk to me in our own home about this and now you want me to seduce you. I'm not going to." She begins walking away.

Where has my power gone? Where is the strong, sexy woman I cultivated before moving here? I was never like this, not even with my ex. How have I slipped into such apologetic living?

"Wait. Ruann," I call, but she is already heading back toward the small room off the hall.

I run and grab her arm as her hand wraps around the door handle. Desperately wanting to keep her from stepping back into that room, I try to speak. My mouth moves without voice and my hold on her weakens. I can't find anything to say. Disgusted, she shakes my arm off and walks into the room, closing the door.

"Damn her!" My heat rises. "Damn her!" I mutter, storming around the hot tub while women I know, more than I want to, watch me. I'm sure they overheard the exchange. The crushed velvet thickness absorbed none of our words or my angst. Lisa leans out over the edge of the hot tub.

"Hey, you, come on in here."

"I'm too hot as it is."

"You sure are," a stranger replies, her straw-colored hair swirling from the tub's jets.

Everyone laughs, except me. I stop pacing, look at Lisa, the unknown woman, and the others in the tub. Lisa's eyes are full of love for me. These people know what I foolishly thought was kept in by the walls of our tiny blue board house. They know what was never spoken between Ruann and me.

"Go on in there, honey. Do what you have to do," Lisa says. "She wants you more than anyone here." I don't trust this southern woman's drawl or her gentle directive. I don't trust myself to go into that room with the closed door.

Lisa continues, "I tried, but." She shrugs.

My throat goes dry. Women are hitting on Ruann. Lisa tried. When? Lisa's playful seriousness, her acquiescence, means that Ruann said no. It doesn't mean Ruann will say yes to me, but there's still a possibility. I breathe as deeply as I can, feel the earth's energy rise in me, and walk to the room that holds my fate. If I slow or linger, I won't do it. I open the door to see three bodies naked, tangled. They look up, surprised. Ignoring the two other women—our best friends, Ginny and Rita—I focus on Ruann.

"I want you," I say, allowing the door to shut or not behind me. It can make up its own mind.

"I want you," I repeat, as I near the edge of the mat.

With her sudden withdrawal from Ruann, Ginny's red hair slips across gray eyes that are waiting to see what I will do. Rita is not so quick to take her hands off Ruann's naked, sculpted body. Rita's nails, a shocking pink, are a magnet attempting to sway my gaze. I ignore their boisterousness, their oddness against Ruann's sunburned skin. I want to be angry, but can't be. Ruann has been looking for closeness and I couldn't, or wouldn't, be there.

Ruann's leg is thrown over Rita's heavy thigh, swollen lips slightly exposed. She is dripping wet, her pubic hair pressed flat against her mound. I bend over, put my face directly in front of Ruann's, and ask, "Do you still want me?"

"Yes."

Our lips meet fiercely as I ease her onto the mat. Rita and Ginny stay close by, watching while making room for me.

I hear Ginny say, "That's it, sweetie. You tell her. You do her real good."

Rita's heart-shaped face and tanned, honey-brown skin lie behind and beyond Ruann's nearness.

"I want you," I whisper into Ruann's ear as I open my mouth along her neck, smoothing my way to her shoulder, dark with Rita's hair. The taste of sweat and sex makes my tongue bead. Rita's long and tangled strands, jet black, tickle my face as I nuzzle into Ruann's heaving body. Her breath hasn't slowed since I stormed in. I feel a pair of hands running up my back and tense at the unexpected touch. The distraction shuts down my wanting.

"We're just going to help you two. Don't worry." Ginny's words hold me as she slips off my shirt before gently resting me on Ruann's breasts. Massaging, Ginny's tender hands entice sensations forgotten.

"Sit up a bit, sweetie," Rita instructs Ruann as Rita slips underneath our body web. She brings Ruann's head down against her chest with satisfied encouragement. I watch Ruann lean completely into this woman and let myself follow. Breathing in the scent of Ginny behind me, the scent of sex all around me, I relax into Ruann. Ginny kneads my back, dipping down my spine, releasing every bound muscle and emotion. Ruann's sea-green eyes slide down me, a mirror of Ginny's hands. Instead of tensing against her, instead of fighting, I melt into the tangle.

Rita's hands, calloused and broad, explore our arms. She moves from Ruann to me back to Ruann as if our arms are one long continuous line. Rita murmurs sweet sounds that fill my ears and are echoed like gentle waves lapping on the stone beach bay by our home.

"I haven't heard you make those sounds in four years," Ruann says to me. I hadn't heard—or recognized—myself.

"God, I'm sorry. I'm sorry." The words tumble out of me, smoothing the jagged edge between us, crumbling the interior walls. She strokes my head.

"I know."

I run my cheek across hers, first one side, then the other. Her skin is like silk. My cheek slides along her neck, around her breasts, over her nipples. Rita rocks us. Ginny slips her hands into my jockeys and pulls them down. Up on my knees to help her undress me, I rest calves between Ruann's legs, face against her breast. I slowly spread my legs, pushing Ruann's farther apart. Will she want more sex? She has already been filled tonight.

"Use this," Ginny instructs, handing me Ruann's favorite vibrator. I run its trembling head against the inside of Ruann's thigh and bring it to her clit. She falls heavily onto the sturdy and constant woman behind her, body completely soft so that she can continue being pleasured. Her willingness to give herself up, to receive, be held, be touched—it stuns me. I am so afraid to surrender. What would be left of me if I gave myself over? An unexpected thought flashes through my mind, scaring me, but it sticks.

Perhaps she's not giving herself up.

I feel the revelation, tangible, tiny, and amorphous, lodge

mysteriously in my body. Watching Ruann unfold, I want to know how she does that. I want to feel it.

What I feel is a slippery cool dribble down my ass, between my cheeks, and then an intense opening as Ginny enters my anus. Her finger doesn't penetrate far, but far enough. She moves her knees between my own and spreads my legs, Ruann's legs, Rita's legs, and then slides a dildo inside me. Ruann, humming to her vibrator, smiles when I breathe in this woman's entry, as if she, Ruann, can feel the entry too.

"Are you finding yourself again, baby?" The words drift from behind me.

Is this me—this feeling? If it is me, it's a part I have never met. I feel full and lost and shaken. I have to close my eyes to shut everything else out. My vertebrae, one by one, are running together, aligning themselves with every thrust from this woman behind me. Sensations radiate like veins on a leaf across my back. One pulsing vein reaches around my side and wraps around my heart. Another snakes into my lungs, up through my trachea, where it slides between teeth and hisses with its release. Others grow like vines around my intestines and stomach and liver, enveloping and bringing together parts that believed themselves separate. My uterus tightens, loosens, tightens like I am expelling a baby and lets go a flood of red waters. My legs shake as my head swims. I feel a rush of energy from far below my feet cresting as it passes through me. The wave carries with it the flooding red, the entwining green, the slithering and pulsating. Unknowable sounds gurgle out of my mouth. Ruann takes them into her own mouth, swallowing them whole.

I am so full that I am weighted down, so empty I cannot hold myself up. I crumble, once again, dissolving on top of Ruann as I come, her vibrator hard between us. Rita slides back and rests to the left of us. Ginny slips out, curling around to our right. They surround us with soft skin and breasts and folds of women's flesh. We are holding each other, unwilling to move. I drift in and out of consciousness with questions swirling in my head. Why did I stay away, hidden for so long? Are these walls gone? What was I so scared of?

Reaching out to touch Ginny and Rita I say, "I'm glad it was you. Thank you."

"Sweetheart, you don't have to thank us. You know we'd do anything for our friends." Ginny's voice, casual but pleasure-laden and satisfied, makes it sound as if they had picked up milk at the corner store when we ran out. As if opening us up, bringing us together—as if this intimacy—is an everyday occurrence. Laughter at her offhandedness shakes through me, jiggling loose the last of my belly tightness. I know it is true. They would do anything for their friends. They did.

"Coming inside, sugar?"

Ruann's words float out of the steaming kitchen on the scent of jasmine and cinnamon.

"I will. Soon," I call back, relaxing into the darkening fog.

The mist tonight is making me grateful to our friends. Not just for what they did for Ruann and me, but because now I love the feel of soft pillow caves, and flesh and fat and mist surrounding me. The hands holding mine are no longer just Ruann's. I don't have to fight comfort anymore, and I still love the feel of unfiltered sun on my skin. There is room for both. Surprisingly, nothing is lost.

From Barbie to Bootie
Jera Star

Ricky and I have been best friends for years. From playing Barbie to stealing lipstick. From first kisses (hers for ten
seconds in the back of a closet with the most popular boy in
class, mine for ten minutes behind the portable with tomboy
Jane) to first highs. From matching thongs to color-coordi-
nated vibrators. She comes to dyke events with me as the
"sexy straight girl," and says no when the butch girls ask
her to dance. I go to straight bars with her as the "big-busted
lesbian" and turn down the bio boys who want to grind. She
tells me stories about the guys she does, the size of their cocks,
what she likes them to do to her. I tell her about the boydykes
I bring home on weekends, the size of my cock, what they like
me to do to *them*. She asks me what it's like to wear a strap-
on. I wonder what it's like to suck on a real cock. Ricky and I
share clothes, boots (fuck-me or shit-kicker, depending on the
day), and cigarettes. But never, not ever, have we fucked.

Which is why, on waking this morning, flush from a dream
of her and me in the throes of a sixty-nine, I was shocked. I
jumped right out of bed and into the shower to try to wash it

away. But it was all I could do to keep from touching myself right there under the running shower, and later on the drive to work, and on every bathroom break at work....

By the time dinner is made and I am watching her walk up the path to my door for our weekly dinner, I decide to give in to my desire. Why have I never before thought of Ricky as a potential lover? Right now I can think of no good reason. She does look good in those jeans.

"Hi, Sue," she says, coming through the door smiling. She gives me her usual French peck-on-the-cheek hello.

I think about the stories my butch lovers have told me of how their charm has seduced hardcore straight girls out of the closet and into their beds. I worry for a second that I might have to play butch to do the deed of wooing Ricky. Get cozy in my old cargo pants and baseball hat, and practice my swagger.

"Hi," I reply, giving her the warm hug I usually offer.

I wonder if my face goes bright red, or if I am already blushing—memories of the dream so close to the surface of my skin. My cunt is newly aware of how her tight jeans hug her femme ass when she bends over to take off her shoes. I can't help myself, I move my hand down my own large, tight-skirted, femme ass. A perfect red mini, which I put on after my shower, wore shamelessly all day at work, and kept on while I made dinner and waited for Ricky to get here.

"Nice skirt," Ricky says, sliding her hands from my hips down my red velvet thigh.

I decide my femmeness will be more than enough charm.

"Which reminds me!" she says, passing me by and heading toward the stairs. "I've got a big date tomorrow night with Mike. I've got to borrow something."

"Half the stuff in my closet is yours already, you know!"

I follow her up the stairs and right away she is skinning off her jeans and donning a black leather skirt I assume she's brought to try on with my clothes for her date. I recognize the skirt. She often wears this particular skirt on special occasions.

"So what's so special about this date with Mike?" I ask, trying not to show my jealousy, wondering how I'm going to get her mind off him.

She doesn't answer me but picks up a black button-up blouse of mine and asks, "What do you think?"

I shake my head no and lie on my bed while she picks out a couple more shirts and tries them on. For the first time ever it feels strange to have her baring her breasts in front of me. OK, not strange, it feels hot. Fucking hot. Who'd have thought, after all these years of butches and bois, I'd be getting wet over my straightest girlfriend?

"I wish my boobs could fill out this thing like yours can," she says, talking about my leopard print bodice.

"I've got an idea." I open a drawer in my dresser and take out some clear packing tape.

"What are you going to do?"

"I'm going to give you cleavage."

"Cleavage?" she asks skeptically.

"Oh, yes."

The tape makes a loud tearing sound as I pull the first bit away from itself. I don't tell her that I've never tried this to actually make cleavage before, only to make my butch lover's breasts disappear when they want to feel more like boys. I do tell her to take off my shirt, which she is wearing. She does, without hesitation.

"Lift up your arms...higher."

I start the tape on her left side and pull it around her back and then across her front, lifting her breasts as I do. When I look up at her, she seems a little embarrassed, a little curious. On the next time around her body, the tape pushes up on the underside of her small breasts. Around again and again it does this even more. I am careful as it goes higher, to make sure the tape pushes her breasts together from the outside and up from underneath. Finally, an inch or so under the nipple, I tear away the last bit of tape with my teeth. She smiles as she watches me. Her breasts are squeezed together high and tight, and hard nipples perk out over the top of the tape.

I put one hand on her waist and casually brush my other hand against her nipples as I turn her around to face the full-length mirror. She moves her hands from above her head to linger, first, on the tape that holds her breasts high, then down to rest just on top of mine. Her pinkies touch my thumbs. She looks at me in a way that makes me believe I've got her. It's working. I can feel her heartbeat quickening. Or is it my own? Her new cleavage rises and falls. I let her watch me watch her in the mirror, slowly moving my eyes from her naked feet, up her thighs, over her skirt, along her waist to her bound torso and hard nipples, across her bare shoulders, down her arm to her smooth hand that is now reaching back to touch me. And then I freeze.

It is a strange feeling to know that you are in control of a seduction, in a way only a femme can be. That you have the power to make your seductee come to her knees in desire, at just the moment you wish. That you can tell when you're making her nervous, making her curious. When you're making her need to move a little bit closer to you and brush her body against yours. When you're making her want to touch your bare forearm, your short-skirted thigh. That you know when she's ready for it, before she does. That you make her ready.

It's an even stranger feeling to believe that you are in control of a seduction, until, at a point much too late in the game to reclaim it, you realize it is she who is seducing you. In a way only a femme can do. That she has had the power all along. That she knows she has made you nervous and curious and hot and wanting. Has made you want to press your bare arms against hers. Has made you want to clutch her short-skirted thigh. Has made you ready to come to your knees in desire. And knows you will do so at just the moment she wishes.

It's her nails. She has cut her nails.

I look at her in the mirror again, eyebrows raised. She smiles coyly, turns around, keeping my hands on her hips, and stands so that her nipples and mine are touching. She takes my hand and slides it from her hip down her thigh to the bare skin just below the hem of her skirt.

My fingers curl up under the hem. Then she makes me lift it up a couple of inches. I catch my breath. Something long and hard presses into my red velvet skirt. With her free hand she touches my cheek and takes a small step toward me so her lips are a mere inch from mine. Her nipples press harder into mine. I know it is my own dildo's head poking out from just under Ricky's skirt.

My hands slide up from her ass to her waist, to the edge of her bound and perked breasts, thumbs resting on the tape just an inch away from her nipples.

"Gotcha," she says before she kisses me.

I stumble backward onto the bed beneath her. The space between my thumbs and her nipples disappears. I play with her nipples and bring her to stand between my legs while I sit on the edge of the bed. Kiss her neck, her waist. Surround her strong red nipples with my mouth. When I do, her head stretches back and she moans. I go back and forth between her nipples, flicking them with my tongue until she is so turned on that she grabs her new cock with one hand and pushes me from the bed to the floor so I am kneeling directly in front of her.

"Suck it, bitch," she says to me, looking very serious for a second. Then she smiles. "Fuck, I've always wanted to say that."

I smile at her obediently and do as told. I lick the length of her dick and slide my hands down her hips below her skirt, and then up and under to her ass, clutching it. My mouth waters and goes around the tip of the thick shaft. Ricky's eyes light up. I start sucking it, one hand around its length, my mouth thrusting. My thong is soaked in seconds. Never before have I enjoyed sucking cock as much as this one under Ricky's special black skirt. Femme power. I know she's getting off on it for the first time.

Eventually, she takes my chin in her hand and brings me to a standing position again. But before I realize it, I'm on my back on the bed, my legs are spread so my skirt rides up around my waist, and Ricky is running her hands up my thighs. First, she teases me by pulling on my wet thong but not touching my cunt. I lift my ass in the air to show her that I want more. As her hands slide together under my ass to pull off my thong, her mouth comes close to my cunt. Her nipples, still hard, brush my thighs. She kneels between my legs and hikes up her own skirt. Grabbing some lube, she drips some onto me. I buck at the cold until she pushes her fingers against my clit to warm it again. Then she starts to play. My cunt opens and closes in time to her fingers on my clit. As she pumps my clit she drips some lube onto her cock and I moan in anticipation.

"So, any advice for the first–timer, Sue?" she asks.

I have a hard time putting together a response because she is still playing with my swollen clit. She sets the dick just at the outside lips of my cunt. It takes everything in me not to push myself onto her. I make myself wait. Her hips, very slowly, nudge it farther into me. I look at her through glazed eyes.

"Just…"

She moves her free hand up her body over the tape to her nipples and starts playing with them. I watch her finger her own nipples until I am completely saturated. She takes her hand away and rests it beside my head, bending over me, pushing slightly farther into me, her hand still on my clit, speeding up. Faster. I am getting closer and closer to coming.

"...fuck me!"

In unison we thrust, and the whole size of her goes into my cunt hard and fast as I come. She thrusts over and over and the waves of orgasm peak, and then peak again and then peak again before finally subsiding.

Ricky lies on top of me, both of us breathing heavily, my tank top soaked with sweat. We stay like that for a while and then she slowly pulls out of me.

"Please tell me, Ricky," I say, "why the hell we never did that before?"

"I thought you were only into butches."

"I thought you were only into boys."

"Well," she says. She slides her hand underneath the strap-on to her cunt and smiles at me. "Apparently not. I'm so fucking turned on, I don't think I could get any wetter."

I smile and kiss her and push her gently onto her back. "Wanna bet?"

She raises her eyebrows.

I slide my skirt back down my thighs, take off my tank top, and leave my bra on but my breasts exposed. I kiss her throat and beautifully bound cleavage and slide down between her legs. I unfasten the strap-on from her waist and throw it aside. Then I lick her stomach and lick her thighs. I move my fingers through her pubes. I grab the leather of her skirt and caress the lips of her wet, wet cunt, slowly pushing one, then two fingers inside, reaching up to her G-spot. She takes a sharp breath as I thrust gently. I put my mouth on her already very swollen clit and start licking.

"Holy shit," she says.

I keep thrusting my fingers into her cunt and sucking on her clit.

Her moans become deeper and more guttural as I fuck her. Faster and harder, pushing against the soft, sensuous part of

her cunt. Licking her clit to the same rhythm. It doesn't take
long before she's practically screaming. Until I feel the inside
of her cunt swell up and her clit take on a life of its own. Until
she's moaning like I've never heard before and my hand and
chin are being soaked by the juice that's coming out of her.

"Sue," she screams. "Sue, Sue, oh my god."

"You okay?" I ask.

"I'm fucking amazing," she says. "Hold me, fuck, hold me.
And promise me one thing."

"What's that?"

"We'll do this all over again tomorrow night."

About the Authors

TONI AMATO has been a teacher, editor, and writing coach since 1992. Most recently, he served as editor for the anthology *Pinned Down by Pronouns*. He has published fiction in several anthologies, including *Best Lesbian Erotica* (1998–2001). "A Perfect Fit" is his first porn story after a four-year hiatus. His newest mission is to promote admiration and plain good old-fashioned lust for fat girls everywhere.

S. BEAR BERGMAN is a theater artist, writer, instigator, and gender-jammer. Ze has toured hir award-winning shows *Ex Post Papa* and *Clearly Marked* around the country to colleges, universities, and theater festivals, including the National Gay and Lesbian Theater Festival and the National Transgender Theater Festival. Ze has been heard and published in a variety of places, lives on the web at www.sbearbergman.com, and makes a home in Northampton, Massachusetts, where ze is the very lucky husbear of a magnificent femme.

BETTY BLUE developed a passion for hot lesbians during her formative years in the Tucson desert, eventually running away in a U-Haul to San Francisco to look for one of her very own. Her fiction has appeared in *Best Lesbian Erotica, Best Women's Erotica, Best Lesbian Love Stories, Tough Girls, Anything That Moves, Best Bisexual Erotica,* and *Best of Best Lesbian Erotica 2.*

CHEYENNE BLUE combines her two passions in life: writing travel guides and erotica. Her stories have appeared in editions of *Best Women's Erotica, The Mammoth Best New Erotica, Best Lesbian Erotica, Best Lesbian Love Stories,* and *Foreign Affairs: Erotic Travel Tales,* and on various websites. Her travel guides have been jammed into many glove boxes underneath the chocolate wrappers. You can see more of her work at www.cheyenneblue.com.

BARBARA BROWN considers traveling the interlocking canals of desire, sexual activity, relationship, and emotion to be central to her being. She is a Toronto-based writer, artist, and integrative craniosacral-psychotherapist. Her publications include *ReCreations* and *Hot and Bothered 3* and *4* (all Lambda Literary Award finalists) and *Journal of Lesbian Studies.* She is also the editor of *My Breasts, My Choice: Journeys Through Surgery,* a photographic and narrative project exploring experiences of breast and chest surgery.

RACHEL KRAMER BUSSEL is a senior editor at *Penthouse Variations,* and writes the Lusty Lady column in the *Village Voice.* She is the editor of *Naughty Spanking Stories from A to Z* and coeditor of *Up All Night: Adventures in Lesbian Sex.* Her writing has been published in more than fifty erotic anthologies, including *Best Lesbian Erotica* (2001, 2004, and 2005) and *Best American Erotica 2004,* as well as *AVN, Bust,*

Curve, Diva, Girlfriends, On Our Backs, Penthouse, Punk Planet, Rockrgrl, the *San Francisco Chronicle, Velvetpark,* and other publications. Learn more about her at www.rachel-kramerbussel.com.

L. SHANE CONNER loves women, but most especially her lover, who is an absolute inspiration. She plays rugby, which is sometimes inspirational, and her teammates are definitely a great source of ideas. She used to say that when she grew up she wanted to write a novel, but she has reevaluated the value of growing up in terms of creativity, and thinks she'll have to try writing one sometime soon.

MARÍA HELENA DOLAN nurtures both tropical plants and subversion across the Atlanta area. She has a long history of political and cultural activism, as well as writing. Middle age hasn't stopped her, but it has allowed this self-avowed "co-erotic, technophiliac, wild-eyed, Liberty-login, Latina Dyke" to take the long view on burning issues. She lives with two feline supremacists, a nonalpha dog, and her sometimes-astonished spousal unit.

NIPPER GODWIN is a genderqueer, polyamorous, bisexual switch, born in the Bronx, raised by wolves, educated by the Seven Sisters, and currently dedicated to keeping as many plates spinning at one time as is humanly possible. Godwin's work has appeared in *Best of On Our Backs II* and *Rode Hard, Put Away Wet,* an anthology of lesbian cowboy erotica.

SACCHI GREEN writes in western Massachusetts and the mountains of New Hampshire. Her work has appeared in five volumes of *Best Lesbian Erotica* and four of *Best Women's Erotica,* as well as *Penthouse, Best S/M Erotica 2, Best Transgender Erotica,* and a thigh-high stack of other anthologies with inspirational covers. She is co-editor of *Rode Hard, Put Away Wet: Lesbian Cowboy Erotica.*

EVA HORE is a writer of erotica living down under, in Melbourne, Australia. She has had more than a hundred short stories published over the last two years in places such as *Hustler, Forum, The Hot Spot, New Woman, The Score Group, Swank, Playgirl, Ghedes Books, Afternoon Delights,* and many others. Her first novel, *Sexual Deception,* and two novellas are all due for release with *eXtasy Books* in Canada in 2005.

THEA HUTCHESON burns up the pages with lust, leather, and latex and brims over with juicy bits in *Best Lesbian Erotica* (2001 and 2002), *Cthulhu Sex Magazine,* and *Hot Blood XI* and on Amatory-Ink.com. She's a member of the Northern Colorado Writers Workshop, living in economically depressed, unscenic, nearly-historic Sheridan. When she's not hard—or wet—at the computer, she teaches and reads Tarot.

LYNNE JAMNECK is a writer and photographer from South Africa. Her work has been published in a number of diverse places, including *Best Lesbian Erotica 2003, H. P. Lovecraft's Magazine of Horror, Harrington Lesbian Fiction Quarterly,* and *On Our Backs.* Her first Samantha Skellar mystery will be available in 2005. She is the editor and creator of *Simulacrum: The Magazine of Speculative Transformation.* A raging homo, Lynne currently lives in New Zealand with her delectable girlfriend, looking for lesbian elves.

TENNESSEE JONES is an Appalachian-born transman living in Brooklyn, New York. He is the author of the zine *Teenage Death Songs.* His first book, *Deliver Me from Nowhere,* is available from Soft Skull Press; the collection explores the sex and gender badlands of small-town America through the prism of Bruce Springsteen's *Nebraska*. His work has appeared in numerous publications, including *Lodestar Quarterly* and *Lit*. The flask in his back pocket reads "Hungry Heart."

ROSALIND CHRISTINE LLOYD's work has appeared in *Best Lesbian Erotica 2003, Best American Erotica 2001, Hot and Bothered 1* and *2, Faster Pussycat, Skin Deep,* and *Set in Stone,* among other erotica series. Currently working with a women's nonprofit organization, this womyn of color, native New Yorker, and Harlem resident lives with one unruly feline (along with her own unruly kitty) while obsessing over her first novel.

SKIAN MCGUIRE is a working-class Quaker leatherdyke who lives in the wilds of western Massachusetts with her dog pack, a collection of motorcycles, and her partner of twenty-two years. Her work has appeared in *Best Lesbian Erotica, Best Bisexual Erotica 2, The Big Book of Erotic Ghost Stories,* and *On Our Backs,* and on a variety of webzines. A champion of Boston's Amazon Slam, she has had slam poems published in *Pinned Down by Pronouns* and *I Do/I Don't: Queers on Marriage.*

ELAINE MILLER is a Vancouver leatherdyke who spends her time playing, learning, educating, performing, and writing. Her work has appeared in *Skin Deep II, Brazen Femme,* many of the *Best Lesbian Erotica* series, *On Our Backs, Paramour, Anything That Moves, The No SafeWord Anthology,* and quite a few tawdry porn sites. She writes a regular column for both the *Xtra West* newspaper and *Desire,* a new magazine for Canadian lesbians.

JACK PERILOUS is a New York journalist whose work has appeared in *Best Lesbian Erotica 2003, Glamour Girls:*

Femme/Femme Erotica, The Time Out New York Guide to Bars and Clubs, and *The Rough Guide to New York City,* among other titles. She writes for the gay and lesbian press and contributes regularly to the *Village Voice, Girlfriends, Curve, Lambda Book Report, On Our Backs, POZ,* and *Heeb.*

JEAN ROBERTA teaches first-year English classes at a Canadian prairie university. Since she first loaned a sexually explicit lesbian story to a friend (blush), who later returned it in shreds, her erotic stories have appeared in more than twenty anthologies, including *Best Lesbian Erotica* (2000, 2001, 2004, and 2005). Her reviews and editorials can be found at the websites *Blue Food, The Dominant's View, Clean Sheets,* and in the print journal *Batteries Not Included.*

ALISON SMITH's memoir, *Name All the Animals,* was published by Scribner in 2004. *Name All the Animals* is a Barnes & Noble Discover book and is short-listed for the 2004 Borders Original Voices prize. Her stories and essays have appeared in *McSweeney's, Best American Erotica,* the *London Telegraph, Best Lesbian Erotica,* and other publications. She lives in Brooklyn, New York, and can be reached at www.namealltheanimals.com.

JERA STAR is fond of purple dicks, wooden spankers, and playing Scrabble. Her erotica appeared in *Best Lesbian Erotica 2004.*

DIANE THIBAULT is a French-Canadian butchdyke writer and translator originally from Quebec and now living in Toronto. She enjoys exploring the double-edged sword of sexual identity and expression while quietly subverting the status quo of traditional relationships and mainstream queerness. She has appeared on the television show *Kink II* and dreams of writing the first script for a polyamorous feature film.

RAKELLE VALENCIA has written short stories for Cleis Press, Aphrodite Press, H.A.F. Enterprises, Pretty Things Press, Alyson Publications, and www.sextoytales.com. With Sacchi Green, she is coeditor of the lesbian cowboy erotic anthology, *Rode Hard, Put Away Wet*. She is editing an erotic anthology with the theme of bikers' escapades for Alice Street Editions. See ya between the covers!

VIOLYNTFEMME is a 27-year-old high femme married to the transguy of her dreams, and is pursuing a degree in law. When she isn't slaving away at her day job or school, she can be found sucking down lattes with her nose stuck in a book or writing her smut.

MICHELLE WALSH is a writer and spoken-word artist who has been traveling around the country for the past five years. She is about to move back to San Francisco. More of her work can be found at www.poisonedpunchbowl.com.

SARAH B. WISEMAN's sex stories have appeared in *Faster Pussycats*, *Body Check*, and *Hot and Bothered 3* and *4*. She writes and works as a carpenter in St. John's, Newfoundland.

FIONA ZEDDE is a transplanted Jamaican lesbian who lives and loves in Atlanta. She spends half her days in the city's fabulous feminist bookstore, Charis Books and More, and the other half chained to her computer working on her first novel and an endless collection of smutty stories. Yes, she went to college for that.

About the Editor

TRISTAN TAORMINO is the award-winning author of three books: *True Lust: Adventures in Sex, Porn and Perversion; Down and Dirty Sex Secrets;* and *The Ultimate Guide to Anal Sex for Women.* She is director, producer, and star of two videos based on her book, *Tristan Taormino's Ultimate Guide to Anal Sex for Women 1 & 2,* which are distributed by Evil Angel Video. She is a columnist for the *Village Voice* and *Taboo Magazine.* She has been featured in more than three hundred publications, including the *New York Times, Redbook, Glamour, Cosmopolitan, Playboy, Penthouse, Entertainment Weekly, Vibe,* and *Men's Health.* She has appeared on CNN, *Ricki Lake,* NBC's *The Other Half,* MTV, HBO's *Real Sex, The Howard Stern Show,* The Discovery Channel, Oxygen, and *Loveline.* She teaches sexuality workshops around the country and her official website is www.puckerup.com.